CECIL JARRELL DOWDEN'S
<u>DOPEBOY HUSTLE - THE PLAY</u>

DopeBoy Hustle - The Play

By
Cecil Jarrell Dowden

Order this book online at www.trafford.com
or email orders@trafford.com

Most Trafford titles are also available at major online book retailers.

This is a work of fiction. All of the characters, names, incidents,
organizations, and dialogue in this novel are either the products
of the author's imagination or are used fictitiously.

Printed in the United States of America.

ISBN: 978-1-4269-4445-1 (sc)
ISBN: 978-1-4269-4446-8 (e)

Trafford rev. 12/13/2010

 www.trafford.com

North America & international
toll-free: 1 888 232 4444 (USA & Canada)
phone: 250 383 6864 ♦ fax: 812 355 4082

1) *Calvin Wilkins- A seventeen year old ex-drug carrier/orphan who stills has a drug problem and is trying to straighten up his life and take care of his pregnant girlfriend.*

2) *Briana Parker/Mary Jane- Calvin's seventeen year old pregnant girlfriend who loves him dearly and wants the best for her, Calvin, and their unborn child. (Mary Jane)- The second girl in Calvin's life.*

3) *Kilo- Calvin's ex-drug carrier partner and brother who just got released from juvenile hall after serving a year; Kilo has dreams of establishing himself as a drug dealer and dreams of making his own money and being his own boss.*

4) *Snooky- A wild 28-year old dope fiend who stills lives at home with his mother and has a full time job at McDonalds.*

5) *Baby Dee- A clever kid and part of Kilo's Click; Baby Dee is all about smoking, shooting dice, and making money.*

6) *Lil' Smurf- Another young kid who is part of Kilo's Click; Lil' Smurf also likes smoking, shooting dice, and making money.*

7) *Det. Tyrone Biggs- An ex- drug dealer turned police officer that is trying to help young Calvin turn his life around for the better.*

8) *Ms. Yvette Parker- Briana's mother and a well-educated and strong minded attorney, really hates Calvin because of he was born on the streets and because he got her daughter pregnant.*

9) *Milsap- A crazy crack head who loves smoking, doing crack, and joke around.*

10) *Miss Gloria Parker- Briana's wise and fun-loving grandmother who tells what she knows and really the main person who understand what Calvin has or is going through.*

11) *Sweetchucks- Big Gay Dude in Prison Scene*

12) *Keisha Parker- Briana's smart-mouth, know it all, sixteen year old sister who also hates Calvin and loves to flirt and act wild.*

13) *Damon- Damon is a sneaky guy who wants to get with Briana.*

14) *Officer Buckley- A crooked cop who works under Det. Biggs.*

15) *Tootsie- The dancer at Kilo's Party*

16) *Dr. Perry- The doctor at the hospital*

17) *Officer Ramirez- A tough, lady cop who all about the law.*

SCENE 1
THE DRUG BUST

(Takes place at BRIANA'S House; CALVIN and SNOOKY are sitting on the couch smoking a blunt getting' high as a kite; Then SNOOKY takes a long hit from the blunt)

SNOOKY
(Choking off the blunt)
Yess saa, come to me hey Calvin, this is some good weed mane, I'm bout to kill myself smoking this, I know this ain't that regular green.

CALVIN
Man Snook, that's that Cali kinfolk.

SNOOKY
(holding the blunt)
That light green, you serious

CALVIN
Yeah.

SNOOKY
Hey Cal, how you get a hold of this weed cuz.

(SNOOKY takes another hit)

CALVIN
Rosebud got da hook-up from these white boys from California.

(After CALVIN said that, SNOOKY quickly puts the blunt down and looks at CALVIN)

SNOOKY
You mean this is RoseBud's weed; I don't think we should be smoking this bruh.

(SNOOKY passes the blunt to CALVIN)

CALVIN
What you talking bout Snooky?

(CALVIN takes a hit from the blunt)

SNOOKY
C'mon now Cal, you always smoking up RoseBud's stash, how ya'll gone sell weed and you keep smoking it all.

CALVIN
I don't know Snooky, that's my only problem.

(CALVIN takes another hit from the blunt)

SNOOKY
Aight Smokey, but fo real mane, Kilo gone be mad as hell when he finds out you smoking up RoseBud's stash.

CALVIN
Kilo ain't gone do nothing, besides, I'm just testing it out to make sure it's good, I'm helping us out, bringing us more business, you feel what I'm saying.

SNOOKY
Whateva mane, I'm fittin' head on to work though, today is payday at McDonald's fool.

CALVIN
Well, you gone ahead and pick up that lil' check, you need to get on this dope game cuz, make some real money.

SNOOKY
And let my momma find out, mane you must lost yo mind, Dorothy don't play that, you must forgot how crazy she is.

CALVIN
Oh yeah, she is crazy as hell, well holla at me later on a deal pimp.

SNOOKY
Always cuz, you know I'm you and Kilo #1 customer.

(CALVIN and SNOOKY did their handshake and SNOOKY walks out the door and CALVIN walks toward his room)

(A few seconds later, KILO enters the room with a customer carrying a suitcase who is willing to buy some drugs from him)

BIG BOY
(talking to KILO)
This is a nice spot cuz, it looks familiar, is this that District Attroney's house, Yvette Parker.

KILO
Yeah, my brother talks to her daughter but they're on vacation so we holding this spot down ya feel me.

BIG BOY
Fo' real, well maybe I should come back here sometimes, you know.

KILO
Yeah, but for now, let's get to business.

BIG BOY
You ain't said nothing but a word.

(KILO and BIG BOY walks toward the couch and took a seat; BIG BOY laid the suitcase on the table and KILO then takes out a blunt)

BIG BOY
Oh, you fittin' smoke

KILO
Yeah mane, I always smoke, It brings me good luck.

(KILO blazes it up and starts smoking)

KILO
(smoking the blunt)
You wanna hit

BIG BOY
Nall, let's get this deal out the way first.

KILO
(smoking the blunt)
I'm listening.

BIG BOY
Rumor on the streets is that you and Calvin got a hold of some coke cuz.

KILO
(looking at BIG BOY)
Who told you this?

BIG BOY
Don't worry Kilo, you can trust me, I just wanna buy the whole stash from ya, how does 30G's sound.

KILO
(smoking the blunt)
How it sounds, that sounds too good to be true, but you playin' right.

(BIG BOY opens the suitcase and KILO was shock to find out it was 30 G's laid out in the suitcase; KILO takes one last hit from the blunt and puts it out in the ashtray)

BIG BOY
I'm too old to play games cuz, I'm all about my business.

(Kilo then holds up a stack of money)

KILO
(shock)
I guess it is too good to be true.

(BIGBOY closes the suitcase)

BIG BOY
So, do we have ourselves a deal.

KILO
Do we have ourselves a deal, hell yeah we got a deal, but let me talk it over with my business partner, Hey Calvin, Calvin!

(KILO kept screaming CALVIN's name until CALVIN walks in the room carrying an empty jug)

CALVIN
(carrying the jug)
Hey Kilo, we ran outta kool-aid man and I'm thirsty as hell.

KILO
(talking to BIG BOY)
Hold on for a second cuz

(KILO gets up from the couch and walks toward CALVIN and they huddle up)

KILO
(whispering)
Forget about the kool-aid Calvin, we about to get paid-aid.

CALVIN
What are you talking about Kilo and why are we whispering and who is that?

KILO
(whispering)
Shhhh!, stop talking so loud, you know the cocaine we got a hold off a couple of weeks ago.

CALVIN
Yeah, our side deal that RoseBud wasn't going to know nothing about.

KILO
Yeah, mane this dude is willing to pay us 30 G's for it.

CALVIN
30 thousand, you for real cuz, that coke is only worth 15

KILO
Yeah, we know but he don't know that, I mean we can get paid cuz, I mean get some serious dough.

CALVIN
I don't know cuz, something ain't right about this and plus, don't dude look familiar to you.

KILO
C'mon Cal, stop being so scared.

CALVIN
I ain't scared.

KILO
So what the problem is mane, you know we've been waiting for this moment to come, this is the biggest drug deal we can ever make, this is our chance to branch away from RoseBud and sell drugs for ourselves, like we always talked about, I'm tired of being a drug carrier for dude and I know you are too, we been doing this for 12 years, we know the game, this is our big chance, just think about what you can do with yo share of the money, you can buy your girl Briana all the things she ever wanted.

(CALVIN looks at KILO and then puts his head down and starts thinking for a moment)

CALVIN
Well, since you put it like that, let's make that deal cuz.

KILO
(grinning)
Man, I knew I could count on you, no wonder we're DopeBoyz for life, hey go get the coke so we can make this deal; it's in the suitcase under Briana's bed.

(CALVIN leaves to get the suitcase)

KILO
Well BigBoy, I guess we bout' to make this happen.

BIGBOY
That's good to hear Kilo, cuz I'm all about business baby

(CALVIN comes back with the suitcase)

KILO
(looking at CALVIN)
That's what I'm talking bout', hey Cal, put the suitcase on the table mane and open it so BigBoy can check out the merchandise.

(CALVIN puts the suitcase on the table and opens it and there laid bags fill with cocaine; CALVIN stands over the table)

KILO
So BigBoy, you like what you see.

BIGBOY
You don't mind if I check it out do you.

KILO
All, I don't mind cuz, gone head.

(BIGBOY takes out a bag of cocaine, opens it, put his finger in the bag, took it out and started tasting the cocaine to see if it was good; then he looks back at KILO)

BIGBOY
It's straight, let's make that deal.

(After hearing what BIGBOY said, KILO and CALVIN starts grinning and got excited)

CALVIN
(excited)
Damn, if Snooky was here he would be like Yesss Saaaa, bring on the money.

KILO
(excited)
See Cal, I told you we had nothing to worry about, we bout' to get paid cuz.

(KILO and CALVIN kept saying "We bout to get paid" unit BIGBOY gets up from the couch and ruin the celebration by delivering some devastating news)

BIGBOY
You guys are about to get paid alright, a first class trip to the county jail.

(KILO and CALVIN stop celebrating and look at BIGBOY)

KILO
What you talking bout BigBoy?

(BIGBOY takes off the fake beard and hat and the boys were surprised to find out it was DET. BIGGS)

CALVIN
(shocked)
It's Biggs Kilo, I knew dude look familiar.

DET. BIGGS
(flashing his badge)
Calvin and Kashon Wilkins, you guys are under arrest for possession of drugs, do you boys have anything to say for yourselves.

KILO
A matter of fact I do.

(KILO reaches on his side and takes out a gun and points it right at BIGGS)

KILO
(aiming the gun)
You under arrest for being a pig, do you have anything to say for yourself.

(BIGGS raises his hands in the air; CALVIN is in shock)

CALVIN
(whining)
Hey lo, what's the hell you doing with a gun.

Cecil Jarrell Dowden

KILO (aiming the gun)
What does it look like I'm doing, I'm bout to fix us some pork chops, how you want yours.

DET. BIGGS
(looks at KILO)
Kashon, don't make it worse than it already is.

KILO
(holding the gun)
Keep ya hands up BIGGS, and don't try anything stupid.

(BIGGS kept his hands in the air)

CALVIN
(whining)
Man, this is so messed up cuz, you know what they gone do to us when they catch us, they go put us under the jail for this, we bout to be somebody's bitches bruh, I don't wanna bend over, I don't wanna bend over.

KILO
(aiming the gun)
Stop whining so much Cal, how they go catch us if they don't have a witness.

CALVIN
What you saying cuz?

KILO
(aiming the gun)
What I'm saying, I'm saying I'm bout to smoke this fool, Good bye Biggs.

(Before KILO could pull the trigger on his gun, Police officers RAMIREZ bust through the front door and BUCKLEY came from

*the back behind CALVIN and KILO. The officers ordered KILO
and CALVIN to put their hands up in the air and they did it)*

RAMIREZ
Hey Biggs, are you ok?

BUCKLEY
Yeah man, you straight

DET BIGGS
I'm straight.

(Then BIGGS looks at KILO and CALVIN and smiles)

DET. BIGGS
*15 thousand dollars worth of cocaine and you guys thought you
could get away with this, did you, this is quite a felony charge
you got over your heads my friends, and you think ya'll bad boys
don't ya, well where you guys are about to go, they turn bad boys
into good girls, Ramirez and Buckley, take these guys in.*

*(KILO and CALVIN started yelling at DET. BIGGS as BUCK-
LEY and RAMIREZ carried them to the front door, DET. BIGGS
left out last, carrying the suitcase filled with coke and money)*

CALVIN
(narrates)
*Ain't this something, Kilo and I finally got caught, trying to
make our first deal on our own, I ain't surprise though, it was
bound to happen sooner or later, this dope game is dangerous
kinfolk, you gotta watch who you dealing too and most impor-
tantly who you dealing with, being an orphan you learn these
things, the streets is your home and the dope is your way to
survive, it's all part on my story, my life, and my hustle.*

SCENE 2
BRIANA'S PREGNACY

(A year later, 17 year old CALVIN WILKINS; an ex-drug carrier is now handling his responsibilities of taking care of his pregnant girlfriend BRIANA; it takes place at BRIANA'S home who CALVIN is now living with)

(CALVIN opens the door and enters the house)

CALVIN
(stops at the door and waits a few minutes)
Briana, hurry up baby, you know I can't be waiting for you all day.

BRIANA
(yelling)
I'm coming CALVIN, I'm coming.

(Pregnant BRIANA enters the house breathing very hard)

BRIANA
(breathing hard)
Why do you have to walk so fast, you know that I'm pregnant.

CALVIN
(playing with BRIANA)
Fo' real, you're pregnant, girl why you didn't tell me, and all this time I just thought you were just gaining a few pounds, I was about to put you on a diet, hey who yo baby daddy is.

BRIANA
(still breathing hard)

*All, I see you got jokes don't you, boy help me to the couch.
(CALVIN helps BRIANA to the couch and they both sat down)*

BRIANA
(furious)
I don't think I can make it, this baby is killing me.

CALVIN
You'll be aight Bri.

BRIANA
(yelling at CALVIN)
I'll be aight, is that all you can say to me.

CALVIN
What you want me to say?

BRIANA
*More than you'll be aight, Calvin baby, I'm in a lot of pain, I
just wish boys could become pregnant instead of girls, then you'll
understand what I'm going through.*

CALVIN
*And if that were true; I would be a virgin till this day, you
wouldn't be getting my goodies.*

BRIANA
*All, so you can't picture yourself being pregnant and you call
yourself a man and you can't handle this pain.*

CALVIN
*Hell nall, the thought of a man being pregnant never crossed my
mind, where they do dat at?*

BRIANA
*All jokes aside Calvin, I just wish you could be serious about this
situation you got me in.*

CALVIN
I got you in, what are you trying to say, it's all my fault, I might had laid down that pipe but you had something to do with it, you know you had fun riding this rollercoaster, I handle my business.

BRIANA
Yeah, you did handle yo business and it only took two minutes.

CALVIN
Huh, what you talking bout girl, I see you got jokes.

BRIANA
Ok Cal, but you think you can be serious about this.

CALVIN
I am serious, what, you think I just don't care about what's going on.

BRIANA
(tired)
Calvin, Calvin, just stop it ok, I don't have time for ahhhhhhh!

(BRIANA starts to hold her stomach)

CALVIN
(worried)
Ahhhhhhh, what the hell dat means, Briana, what's wrong, you having the baby, wait here, I'm going to call 911.

(CALVIN jumps off the couch and runs to the phone)

BRIANA
(yelling)
CALVIN!!

CALVIN
(picking up the phone)
Don't worry bay, I got this situation under control, ok, what's the number for 911.

BRIANA
(yelling)
CALVIN!!

CALVIN
(holding the phone)
Hold on Bri; let me think for a second, damn what's that number, man I knew I should have stayed in school.

BRIANA
Calvin, will you please shut the hell up, I'm not having the baby.

CALVIN
(holding the phone)
You're not.

BRIANA
No, we have 3 more months for that, the baby was just kicking, hang the phone up silly.

(CALVIN hangs the phone up and sat back down on the couch beside BRIANA)

CALVIN
(worried)
Girl, don't scare me like that, having me screaming like a white girl, you bout to give me a heart attack.

BRIANA
Give me your hand.

CALVIN
For what, what you want my hand for.

BRIANA
Boy, just give me your hand.

(BRIANA grabs CALVIN'S hand and laid his hand across her stomach)

BRIANA
Can you feel the baby kicking?

CALVIN
(rubbing BRIANA'S stomach)
Dawg, our baby has a strong kick.

BRIANA
That's our baby girl.

CALVIN
Baby girl, nall, that's Calvin Jr. kicking up in there.

BRIANA
But the doctor said that we were going to have a girl.

CALVIN
You know doctors don't know what they talking about half the time.

BRIANA
And you know.

CALVIN
Of course I know.

BRIANA
Whateva Calvin.

CALVIN

But fo' real though, whateva we have, boy or girl, he or she will always have their father's love.

BRIANA
(smiling)
Ah, that's the sweetest thing you ever said to me, I don't think I ever seen your sensitive side before.

CALVIN
I know, I thought I didn't even have one.

(BRIANA starts smiling and CALVIN grabs her hand)

CALVIN
(holding BRIANA's hand)
Listen bay, A lot of things changed about me, Spending six months at boot camp help me realize that the streets can't offer nothing for me, and you end up getting pregnant with my child really open my eyes, I'm tryin' to straighten my life together, I mean, your mom took me in and hooked me up with a job at Pizza Hut, I stopped hanging out with the crew and gave up the dope game, basically, what I want you to know is that I love you and I will always be there for you and my child.

BRIANA
(smiling)
Do you really mean that?

CALVIN
Every word of it, I love you Bri Bri.

BRIANA
Oh, I love you too Calvin.

(CALVIN and BRIANA gave each other a kiss)

BRIANA
I could use a nap, but do you rather come in my room, we can just listen to some music instead.

CALVIN
Nall, you need some rest, I'm just gonna lay back on the couch and watch a lil' tv.

BRIANA
(BRIANA gives CALVIN a kiss, gets up from the couch and leaves)

(When BRIANA leaves, CALVIN gets up from the couch and looks toward where BRIANA walked; then he takes out a blunt)

CALVIN
(talking to the blunt)
Mary Jane, I've wanted to smoke you all day.

(CALVIN took out his lighter, blaze it up, and started smoking while laid back on the couch)

(CALVIN kept on smoking until he heard BRIANA's sister KEISHA and her mother YVETTE PARKER at the door and he quickly put the blunt out and threw it under the couch and put the lighter back in his pocket, took out some spray and start spraying to kill the scent, and pretend he was watching television)

(KEISHA came through the door first singing and dancing while listening to a song on her CD player and then YVETTE PARKER came in the door talking on her cell phone)

YVETTE PARKER
(talking on her cell phone)
Don't worry Clarence, you have a case here, I will do anything I mean anything to make sure that your testimony will be heard. I'll see you in court first thing Monday morning right, Ok then, I talk to you then, ok, bye bye.

(YVETTE PARKER hangs up the phone)

YVETTE PARKER
Whew, if I knew being a lawyer would be this hard I would have changed occupations a long time ago.

CALVIN
(laying on the couch)
Hey Ms. Parker

YVETTE PARKER
Oh, Hey Calvin, I didn't see you there.

(Then YVETTE PARKER looks at KEISHA singing and dancing in the house)

YVETTE PARKER
Keisha, Keisha.

(KEISHA didn't here her momma talking to her and she continue to sing and dance; then YVETTE PARKER walks toward where KEISHA was and snatch the headphones off her head)

KEISHA
(looking at her momma)
What you doing momma?

YVETTE PARKER
(talking to Keisha)
Takeisha Shanelle Parker, what the hell is wrong with you, you having a seizure.

KEISHA
Sorry ma, I was listening to this new Lil' Wayne song, dis song is bumpin.

YVETTE PARKER
Lil' Wayne, is that boy in jail and what you talking bout bumping, let me listen to that.

(YVETTE PARKER puts the headphones on and starts listening to the song; after she hear a few minutes of the song, she takes the headphones off)

YVETTE PARKER
What is this, this is what you kids listen to these days, I can't believe the language that I'm hearing, What is this Keisha.

KEISHA
Music

YVETTE PARKER
No, this is not music, back in the day when we had Marvin Gaye "What's Going On" and Aretha Franklin "R.E.S.P.E.C.T., now that was music, all of this sticking and moving and calling young ladies whores; this is nothing but street trash and I do not want you listening to this junk anymore.

(YVETTE PARKER takes the cd player)

KEISHA
Come on momma, why you trippin.

YVETTE PARKER
Trippin, I'm not falling; I'm standing still, see, that's what wrong with these kids today, listening to this junk is also messing up your vocabulary, well, it won't happen in this house.

KEISHA
What are you trying to say?

YVETTE PARKER
I'm saying this kind of music is not allow in my house, I didn't raise you to be a whore who wanna shake what her momma gave her, I raise you to be a respectful young lady, now do I make myself clear.

KEISHA
Yes ma'am

YVETTE PARKER
Now, since we got that clear, where's your grandmother.

KEISHA
I thought she was with you.

YVETTE PARKER
You thought she was with me.

(MS. GLORIA walks toward the door carrying a bag full of stuff)

MS. GLORIA
(carrying a bag full of stuff)
Excuse me, but can an old woman get a little help over here.

CALVIN
I got ya Ms. Gloria.

(CALVIN gets up from the couch and walks toward MS. GLO-RIA; KEISHA sits on the couch and starts flipping through the channels of the remote and YVETTE PARKER takes a seat in her chair)

CALVIN
Here, let me help you with this stuff.

(CALVIN grabs the bag of stuff from MS. GLORIA except one)

MS. GLORIA
Oh, thank you Calvin sweetie, I always known that I can rely on you.

CALVIN
(carrying the bag of stuff)
Don't mention it, you want me to get that bag from you.

MS. GLORIA
I got it Calvin, you were helpful enough.

CALVIN
You sure.

MS. GLORIA
I'm sure, but that's nice of you for asking, you can just put this stuff in my room sweetie.

CALVIN
Yes ma'am.

(CALVIN leaves; MS. GLORIA sits in her rocking chair)

SCENE 3
PROBLEMS WITH THE PARKERS

(KEISHA, YVETTE PARKER, and MS. GLORIA are in the living room sitting down talking)

MS. GLORIA
What a cute kid?

YVETTE PARKER
He's cute alright, but he's still a thug in my eyes.

(MS. GLORIA looks at her daughter in distract)

MS. GLORIA
Yvette, why you always given that boy a hard time.

YVETTE PARKER
Momma, Calvin was born and raised on the streets, he's a hustler momma and he cannot be trusted, especially now that he stays with us.

KEISHA
Momma's right, he's probably in your room stealing something right now, I'll watch my stuff if I was you Grandma, I'll lock my door every time I leave out the room, even when I walked up the hallway for a second, I don't trust that boy.

MS. GLORIA
I can't believe what I'm hearing, my own daughter and granddaughter talking this way; I'm glad Briana isn't hearing this; It would just break her little heart, do you at least care about her feelings.

YVETTE PARKER
Momma, if it's wasn't for Briana's feelings, Calvin would be in juvenile hall right now alongside his hoodlum brother Kashon, he's lucky he only got six months at boot camp because I really didn't have to help him.

MS. GLORIA
I know all of that Yvette but you have to realize kids make mistakes, Calvin had his up-and-downs and he's trying to change, Just give the boy a chance.

YVETTE PARKER
(frustrated)
Give him a chance, I gave him too many chances Momma and I'm sick of it and I'm sick of you always defending him.

(MS. GLORIA gets up from her rocking chair)

MS. GLORIA
(furious)
What did you just say?

KEISHA
Uh Oh, I don't think you should have said that to Grandma.

MS. GLORIA
Keisha, I think you better leave for a minute.

KEISHA
Why do I have to leave, things are started to get very interesting and its not the show on tv.

YVETTE PARKER
(yelling)
Leave child!

KEISHA
(scared)
Yes ma'am
(KEISHA jumps up from the couch and left; MS. GLORIA walked toward her daughter)

MS. GLORIA
(yelling)
Yvette, I know that you're a little frustrated right now but you better watch your mouth, you might be a grown woman but I can still whoop your ass so play me like you don't know me, I'll get a switch and wear that behind out, you know I will.

YVETTE PARKER
(frustrated)
Momma, you just don't understand, Briana's life is ruin because of him.

MS. GLORIA
Her life is ruin, how is her life ruin, because Calvin got her pregnant, is that what you're trying to say.

YVETTE PARKER
(frustrated)
She's only 17 years old momma, she's just a baby herself, my baby.

MS. GLORIA
No Yvette, she might be 17 but she is not a baby anymore, Now you and I both now that Briana is a very strong and bright young woman. She always get straight A's and she never cause any problems at school. Ok, she's pregnant but her life is not ruin. Briana can make it through this, but she needs love and support from us as her family and also from Calvin, too.

YVETTE PARKER
I wish that we would have gotta that abortion momma.

MS. GLORIA
Now you know I don't believe in abortion Yvette, taking away an innocent life is just gonna make the problem worse, She got herself in this situation and she is going to have to take responsibility, God will help her through this.

YVETTE PARKER
(frustrated)
Whatever you say momma, Calvin will always be a low down thug in my eyes.

(YVETTE PARKER gets up from the chair and walks toward the couch; then she stops and looks back at her momma)

YVETTE PARKER
(talking to her momma)
You know what momma, Calvin has broken the heart that connected this family and there is no way it can ever be fixed.

(Then YVETTE PARKER turns back around and walks pass CALVIN who just enter the room, CALVIN seen how frustrated YVETTE PARKER was looking when she walks pass him; MS. GLORIA sat back down on the couch)

CALVIN
(talking to MS. GLORIA)
Is there something wrong with Ms. Parker?

MS. GLORIA
Nall, there's nothing wrong with her, sit down suga, there are a few questions that I need to ask you.

(MS. GLORIA sat on the couch and CALVIN sat down beside her)

MS. GLORIA
Now, tell me Calvin, and be honest, do you love my grandbaby.

CALVIN

Do I love her, from the bottom of my heart Ms. Gloria, you know I was just in her room looking at her sleeping, she was looking so peaceful, I would do anything for that girl, provide her with the things she needs, and make sure that she is always loved. I will always be there for Briana, I ain't going nowhere. She is my inspiration, she's my everything, and she is the love of my life.

(MS. GLORIA shakes her head up and down)

CALVIN

Why do you ask that Ms. Gloria?

MS. GLORIA

No reason Calvin, no reason at all, but hey can I ask you one more question.

CALVIN

Sure

MS. GLORIA

I'm supposed to be going out with the pastor tonight and like you young people say these days, I'm trying to get me sum tonight, if you know what I mean, and I wanna know your opinion on this.

(MS. GLORIA pulls a pair of thongs out the bag)

MS. GLORIA

I ain't the coke bottle shape I used to be since I got this big old ba-du-ka-du behind me, I still know how to grind baby, I might be old but I got wisdom child.

CALVIN

(Pauses for a second)
Well Ms. Gloria, they say age ain't nothing but a number, if you act young, you still young.

MS. GLORIA
(holding the thongs)
You know what, I was thinking the same thing, I'm gonna make that man scream "hallelujah, Thank ya Jesus, Amen, we gone have our own little bedroom sermon tonight, whewww, let me stop I'm getting myself hot just thinking about it.

(MS. GLORIA puts the thongs back in the bag)

MS. GLORIA
Have you eaten today Calvin, you want me to fix you something.

CALVIN
Nall, I don't wanna cost you any trouble of fixing me something to eat.

MS. GLORIA
I don't mind sweetie, let's go to the kitchen and I'll fix you some of my famous sweet potato pie.

CALVIN
Ok

(CALVIN gets up from the couch)

MS. GLORIA
Sweetie, can you help an old woman up, my legs are not like they use to be.

CALVIN
Yes ma'am.

(CALVIN helps MS. GLORIA up from the couch and they both walk into the kitchen)

SCENE 4
KILO'S RELEASE

(Takes place in front of the juvenile hall faculty and SNOOKY,
BABY DEE, and LIL' SMURF and listening to the radio while
waiting for KILO to be released from juvenile hall. BABY DEE
and LIL' SMURF are in the backseat while SNOOKY is behind
the wheel.

BABY DEE
(moving his head to the music)
Hey Snooky, cut the music up mane.

SNOOKY
Mane you crazy, we're in front of a police station.

BABY DEE
And…, those cops ain't bout nothing.

SNOOKY
Aight, and when they put us in jail they still won't be bout nothing won't it. I ain't trying to mess up my probation and have my
momma actin' a damn fool, hell nall.

LIL' SMURF
Mane, I can't believe Kilo is getting out, it's been a year already.

BABY DEE
It really don't seem like it been a year.

SNOOKY
Mane, if he don't hurry up he gone have to stay in here another
year, I'm ready to smoke.

LIL SMURF
You ready to smoke, you just got through smoking a blunt Snooky.

SNOOKY
That's was 30 minutes ago Smurf, you know I have to smoke weed every 30 minutes for my weedly diet.

BABY DEE
Mane, you ain't nothing but a crackhead.

SNOOKY
Hey Baby Dee, how many times do I have to tell you, I smoke weed, I don't do crack ok, Crack is Wack ok, that's what Whitney Houston said, Crack is Wack and Weed Indeed, that's my motto, remember that.

LIL' SMURF
(looking out the window)
Hey, shut up ya'll, here comes Kilo.

BABY DEE
(looking out the window)
Fo' real.

SNOOKY
It's about time.

(SNOOKY takes out a blunt, blazes it up, and starts smoking it.

LIL' SMURF
(looking out the window)
Hey Snooky, put that blunt out.

SNOOKY
(smoking)
For what, I just started smoking it.

LIL' SMURF
It's Biggs dawg.

SNOOKY
Biggs, where.

LIL' SMURF
Escorting Kilo out of the building

SNOOKY
Fo' real dawg, just when I was about to get blazed, let me cut the music off.

(SNOOKY cuts the music off and put the blunt out)

SNOOKY
Hey Smurf and Dee, you know what, Biggs might escort him to the car, hey do it smell like I been smoking.

LIL' SMURF
What da hell you think bruh, you smoke 3 blunts on our way up here.

SNOOKY
I can fix that problem.

(SNOOKY takes out a bottle of air freshener and starts spraying it; BABY DEE and LIL' SMURF starts coughing and yelling that too much spraying; SNOOKY stops spraying)

SNOOKY
(takes a deep breath)
Smell that air guys, it's that lemon scent smell.

(KILO and DET. BIGGS enters)

> KILO
>
> *You can go now Det. Biggs, my ride is right over there.*

> DET. BIGGS
>
> *And…I ain't stopping you.*

> KILO
>
> *You know what Biggs, why you still sweating me, I already served my year.*

> DET. BIGGS
>
> *And it's a year too early, you haven't changed a bit, haven't you, you're still the same old young hoodlum that likes starting trouble, I can tell.*

> KILO
>
> *Man whateva.*

(When KILO was about to walk off, DET. BIGGS grabs KILO by the arm)

> DET. BIGGS
> *(holding Kilo's arm)*
>
> *Listen to me Kashon, Don't start any trouble, I don't wanna hear about you dealing drugs on the streets again. I mean, you got a second chance at life, don't make the same mistake again. You're 18 years old, do something with your life.*

(KILO snatches his arm back)

> KILO
>
> *Man you better get your hands off me before I file police brutality.*

> DET. BIGGS
>
> *Stay off those drugs Kashon, I mean it, next time you won't be so lucky.*

KILO
Whateva cuz, you need to stay away from those donuts, that's what you need to do bigboy.

(DET. BIGGS walks off and KILO got in the passenger side of the car; the guys greet KILO)

BABY DEE
Hey, how was prison life Kilo, I hope you didn't drop the soap.

(The guys start laughing at KILO)

LIL' SMURF
Yeah, is your name still Kashon or Kashana.

(The guys start laughing at KILO again)

KILO
(grinning)
I see you guys got jokes, My name is Kilo, no more Kashon, hey Snook, start this piece of junk, I'm tired of looking at this place.

SNOOKY
Hey mane, don't be talking bout my Cadillac dawg, next to women and weed, my car is my most prized possession.

(KILO reaches in his pocket and takes out a roll full of money)

KILO
(waving the roll of money in SNOOKY'S face)
This is for gas, now will you start this piece of junk.

SNOOKY
(takes the roll of money and started counting)
Yess saa, come to me, hell with this kind of money, you can have this piece of junk.

33

(SNOOKY starts the car and drove off, KILO takes out some more money and starts counting it)

LIL' SMURF
Dawg Kilo, what'cha been doing in prison.

KILO
You know I had to get my hustle on Smurf, you know how many cats in prison who smoke weed, from the security guards to the cafeteria ladies, I been getting dat money.

LIL' SMURF
I can see that.

KILO
Hey, but that's not all though.

SNOOKY
What else do you got?

(KILO went in his pocket and took out a blunt)

KILO
(holding the blunt)
Look what I got, this that kush right here kinfolk.

SNOOKY
Look at this fool with the blunt, hey let me hit that first kinfolk, I had to put mine out.

LIL' SMURF
Nall, let me hit it first.

BABY DEE
Nall, let me hit it first.

(SNOOKY, LIL' SMURF, and BABY DEE starts arguing about smoking the blunt first but KILO cuts them off)

KILO
Ain't nall one of ya'll hitting this first, I'm bout to get the first hit of this.

(KILO lights the blunt up and starts smoking it)

KILO
(laughing)
Mane I feel so much better now.

SNOOKY
Pass the blunt cuz.

(KILO passes the blunt to SNOOKY and he took a hit and a couple of more)

BABY DEE
Hurry up and pass it Snooky.

SNOOKY
Shut up, just one more hit.

(SNOOKY took one more hit and passes the blunt to LIL' SMURF and he passes it to BABY DEE and so forth)

SNOOKY
Hey Kilo, if you looking for a job cuz, I can put a word in for ya at McDonald's.

KILO
McDonald's

(KILO looks back at BABY DEE and LIL' SMURF and the three of them started laughing; SNOOKY looks at them)

SNOOKY *(looking upset)*
*What ya'll boys laughing at, McDonald's is a good honest job,
they bout to promote me to co-assistant to the assistant manager
and I got a lot of changes in mind.*

KILO
(counting his money)
*That's nice to hear Snooky, I'm proud of ya, but I think I just
might keep my old job; I like the money it makes me, I leave
flippin' burgers to you bruh.*

SNOOKY
*So after all you went through, you still gonna sell drugs, you
must don't know RoseBud in jail.*

KILO
So

SNOOKY
*So, that what yo boss and the biggest drug dealer in town, who
you go sell drugs for now.*

KILO
You're looking at him.

(SNOOKY, BABY DEE, and LIL' SMURF looks at KILO)

BABY DEE
Look at dude boy, bout to come up in the dope game ain't it.

KILO
You got that right Dee.

LIL' SMURF
But how Kilo, where you go get your merchandise from.

KILO
I got connections dawg, I got this dude who hooks me up real nice cuz, that's why I was booming so hard in juve, and now that I'm back on the streets, it's time for me to get back on that dope boy hustle, but this time I'm running things, like that old yo gotti sayin, all I ever wanted to do was live the life.

KILO, SNOOKY, BABY DEE, LIL' SMURF
(rapping)
Money, Drugs, Car, Clothes, Hoes, Bricks, Paints, pounds of dro fo sho, a young nigga livin how he suppose, you know.

(The boys started laughing)

KILO
The good times will get better ya'll, wait till I tell my boy Calvin bout this, it was our dream to run this dope game together, a matter of fact, where my lil' brother at, I'm surprise he ain't with ya'll.

(SNOOKY, BABY DEE, AND LIL' SMURF got quiet for a second)

KILO
Why ya'll boys got quiet all of a sudden, something must happen to my brother.

SNOOKY
Sorry to tell you this bruh, but yo boy Calvin gave up the dope game cuz.

KILO
(shocked)
Say what, and you just now telling me this.

SNOOKY
Hey, I know how close you two are, being brothers and all, you was already locked up, I didn't want to upset ya.

LIL' SMURF
Yeah Kilo, ever since Calvin got out of boot camp and got his old lady pregnant, that dude changed, I mean he don't even hang out with us anymore, dude even got a job at Pizza Hut delivering pizza, now you tell me where they do that at?

KILO
I can't believe what I'm hearing, please tell me you joking.

BABY DEE
No joke mane, Smurf telling the truth, Calvin's a sell out dawg.

KILO
Not my boy Cal, we were supposed to stay in this dope game for life man.

SNOOKY
Things change Kilo.

KILO
All I can't have this happening.

BABY DEE
What you plan on doing cuz?

KILO
Well Dee, I'll pay Calvin a little visit later, but for now, I'm bout to get me a place to crash, get on some females, smoke some weed, and throw a lil welcome home party.

SNOOKY
Yess saa, Bet that up cuz.

(SNOOKY cuts up the radio and they started bouncing to the music as SNOOKY is driving)

SCENE 5
BRIANA'S ADMIRER

(Takes place back over BRIANA'S house, CALVIN and BRIANA are cuddle up on the couch flirting with each other while KEISHA is sitting in the chair watching tv; KEISHA is trying to watch tv but is distracted because of the flirting that is going on in the room)

KEISHA
Can you two get a room or something, you see I'm trying to watch tv.

BRIANA
Sorry Keisha, I didn't know we were disturbing you, maybe we should stop baby.

CALVIN
Yeah, maybe we should, but I don't think I can, you're just so beautiful.

BRIANA
I'm beautiful, just look at me Calvin, I'm 6 months pregnant, I'm fat as hell, just look at my stomach.

CALVIN
Just because your stomach a little bigger don't mean nothing, I think you look even sexier.

BRIANA
Fo' real Calvin, what else do you think about me.

(CALVIN and BRIANA start back flirting with each other)

KEISHA
I can't believe this.

(Then someone knocks on the door, KEISHA looks back at CAL-
VIN and BRIANA and they are still flirting with each other)

KEISHA
Since you two are busy, I guess I'll get the door.

(KEISHA gets up from her sit and walks toward the door and
opens it; There stood BRIANA'S friend DAMON carrying a
book and some notes in his hands; KEISHA starts staring at
DAMON)

KEISHA
(smiling)
Hey Damon

DAMON
Hey Keisha

(KEISHA is still staring at DAMON)

DAMON
So you're going to invite me in.

KEISHA
(shaking her head)
Oh, my bad, come on in.

(Damon walks in)

KEISHA
(flirting with DAMON)
So Damon, what cha been up too?

DAMON
Nothing much, just stopping by to remind your sister about the big history test Mr. Baxter giving us Monday.

BRIANA
History test, I almost forgot, let me go get my books.

(BRIANA gets up from the couch, then CALVIN gets up)

CALVIN
Well, since ya'll fittin' study, I gotta be headin' for work, gotta make that money you know.

BRIANA
Can you bring me something to eat when you get off like some hot wings, cheesesticks, throw in a large meat lover or two?

CALVIN
Damn girl, you just got through eating some chicken from Popeye's.

BRIANA
Please baby, you know I'm eating for two.

CALVIN
I can see that but you know I'll do anything for my baby.

BRIANA
All, that's so sweet.

(CALVIN and BRIANA kiss each other which was making DAMON mad, then BRIANA proceeds to walk CALVIN toward the door and they kiss again before he leaves out the door, After CALVIN leaves, BRIANA walks toward the couch where KEISHA and DAMON are, KEISHA is still flirting with DAMON)

BRIANA
Keisha, Do you have anything to do, Damon and I have to study.

KEISHA
(holding on to DAMON)
You two can study, just act like I ain't even here, isn't that right Damon.

BRIANA
Oh Lord, come on Keisha, take a seat Damon; I'll be back.

(BRIANA grabs KEISHA by the arm)

KEISHA
Bye Damon, see you in my dreams boo.

(DAMON waves back at KEISHA; BRIANA and KEISHA leaves)

(DAMON sits on the couch laid back and comfortable, then he notice a picture of BRIANA and CALVIN on the table by the couch and he picks it up)

DAMON
(looking at the picture)
You know what Briana, you should be with me instead of with that boy Calvin, I don't know what you see in him but all of that will be over with soon, you will be mine.

(DAMON puts the picture back on the table and then BRIANA enters the living room with her notebook; BRIANA then sits on the couch besides DAMON)

BRIANA
I apologize about my sister, she can get a little crazy sometimes.

DAMON
That's alright.

BRIANA
Well, I guess we should start studying if we want to pass this test Monday.

(BRIANA then opens her notebook; DAMON continues to stare at BRIANA which is making her very uncomfortable)

DAMON
You know we could study, or we could do something else.

BRIANA
(confused)
Something like what.

(DAMON claps his hands and the lights in the room went dim and a slow song starts to play)

BRIANA
(confused)
What's going on Damon?

DAMON
Briana, you know that I always wanted you.

BRIANA
Say what.

DAMON
That's right girl, I want you, every since we were little I always had a thing for you.

BRIANA
I don't wanna hurt your feelings Damon, but it just wouldn't work out, I'm pregnant with Calvin's baby.

DAMON
So, I don't care, I can take care of you and your baby.

BRIANA
It don't matter, I'm in love with Calvin.

DAMON
You're in love with Calvin, that fool can't provide you with nothing, but me, I can provide you with everything you need, so come on, stop playing games, you know you want this.

BRIANA
I ain't playing games Damon.

(DAMON grins a little, then grabs BRIANA and tries to make out with her)

BRIANA
(yelling)
Stop it Damon, Leave me alone.

(DAMON is forcing himself harder on BRIANA and she is trying to push him off, then when DAMON starts getting more physical, she kicks him where the sun don't shine; DAMON then falls to the floor)

DAMON
(holding his private area)
Now why you wanna go and do that.

BRIANA
(yelling)
I want you to leave DAMON, get the hell out of my house

(DAMON then gets up from the floor)

DAMON
You want me to leave, fine then, I'm out.

(DAMON walks to the door and then stops)

DAMON
I tell you one thing Briana, when Calvin starts messing up, you know who to call.
(DAMON then opens the door)

BRIANA
Wait Damon.

(DAMON turns back around and then closes the door)

DAMON
(smiling)
I knew you'll change your mind, what is it baby girl.

BRIANA
You forgot your book.

(BRIANA picks up the history book and threw it at DAMON; DAMON, with an angry look on his face, picks up his book and leaves. After DAMON leaves, BRIANA sits back down on the couch and then KEISHA enters the living room wearing some sexy clothes to impress DAMON)

KEISHA
What's going on, what was all that noise, and where's Damon.

BRIANA
He had to leave.

KEISHA
He had to leave, well, isn't he coming back.

BRIANA
I don't think you'll be seeing Damon for a while Keisha, he has women problems.

KEISHA
You mean he has a girlfriend, All man, I got all dress up for nothing.

(KEISHA then leaves; BRIANA, with an upset look on her face, puts her hands over her face)

SCENE 6
PARTY OVER KILO'S

(Takes place over KILO'S apartment, the music is blasting and everyone is having a good time, BABY DEE and LIL' SMURF are on the dance floor dancing with a stripper name Tootsie while KILO and SNOOKY are laid back on the couch smoking)

SNOOKY
(smoking the blunt)
You know what Kilo, life can't get any better than this kinfolk.

KILO
(laid back sippin on some vodka)
Yeah Snooky, I like to live my life to the fullest cuz, smoking on some good green, drinking on some good vodka and having fun with my boys; that's part of life my friend.

SNOOKY
Yess saa, I like how you talking.

KILO
(laid back sippin on some vodka; talking to Dee and Smurf)
Ya'll boys havin' fun.

BABY DEE AND LIL' SMURF
(dancing with Tootsie)
Hell Yeah!!

(The boys kept having fun and enjoying their little party until someone knocks on the door)

KILO
(laid back sippin on some vodka)
Hey Snook, see who dat is bangin on my door, I'm bout to head to the back for a minute

SNOOKY
(smoking his blunt)
Bet but what if it's one time cuz.

KILO
Invite em in, ask if they wanna smoke a blunt or two.

SNOOKY
(grinning)
Aight bra.

(KILO went to the back, Snooky gets up from the couch and walks toward the door, he opens it and the neighborhood crack-head Milsap comes inside singing and dancing)

MILSAP
(shuttering and dancing while talking to SNOOKY)
Uh Oh, Partee ova here.

(MILSAP walks pass SNOOKY and gets on the dance floor and starts dancing and acting a fool; BABY DEE, LIL' SMURF, and TOOTSIE stop dancing and looks at MILSAP; KILO enters back in the living room)

KILO
Can ya'll keep it down up in here a little bit, I'm tryna too....

(Then KILO notices that it was MILSAP)

KILO
All Hell Nall, MILSAP

(MILSAP stops dancing and looks at KILO and the music stops)

MILSAP
(shuttering, looking at KILO)
KILO, all Wa dup kinfolk.......

*(MILSAP ran up to KILO and started hugging and spinning
KILO around, then he puts KILO down)*

MILSAP
(shuttering)
Wa dup fool, Wa dup fool, mane is good to see ya.

KILO
Whateva mane, what you doing here Sap.

MILSAP
(shuttering)
*Nuttin much mane, just stopping by, heard you was out, see you
got dis nice partment and everything, and ohhhh weeeee, I see
dis dime piece right here ya'll got, ya'll boys doing it big.*

KILO
Let's cut it short dawg, what is it that you want.

MILSAP
(shuttering)
Hey cuz, let me borrow two dollas.

KILO
Two dollas.

MILSAP
(shuttering)
*Yeah mane, so I can buy me a ham sandwich or sumthing, I'm
hungry.*

49

KILO
You hungry, I see you haven't changed a bit Milsap, man you
betta get you beggin', shuttering ass up out my place, I ain't givin'
you no money.

MILSAP
(shuttering)
C'mon mane, if you ain't got da money, give me sumthing like
some blow or crack or sumthing.

SNOOKY
(makin' fun of MILSAP)
We got ya on that Sap, we got some mouthwash to blow that bad
breath away and some soap so you can wash da crack of yo ass,
that's the only blow and crack you getting over here.

(EVERYBODY starts laughing)

MILSAP
(shuttering)
Wa you talking bout Snook?

(MILSAP then proceed to smell himself)

MILSAP
(shuttering)
I smell good, do I.

(MILSAP raise his arms up and everybody in the room starts
holding their noses)

MILSAP
(looking at everybody, still shuttering)
What, Jealous

TOOTSIE
(holding her nose)

Hey Kilo, thanks for the party but I have to bounce.

LIL' SMURF
Hey, where you going TOOTSIE.

*(SNOOKY, BABY DEE, and LIL' SMURF tried to prevent
TOOTSIE from leaving but she left anyway)*

BABY DEE
(yelling at MILSAP)
*See what you did Milsap, always messing up something, man put
your arms down.*

(MILSAP puts his arms down)

SNOOKY
*Hey Kilo mane, we fittin' bounce too, but we'll holla at ya later,
when the crackhead leaves.*

MILSAP
(shuttering)
*Crackhead, that wasn't what yo momma said last night when we
did the freak nasty last night.*

*(MILSAP starts dancing and grinding, the comment offends
SNOOKY)*

SNOOKY
Say what, what you say bout my momma.

*(SNOOKY was about to attack MILSAP on that comment until
MILSAP ran behind KILO; BABY DEE and LIL' SMURF
grabs SNOOKY, pulling him toward the doorway)*

SNOOKY
*Hey Sap, you betta keep my momma name out yo mouth, Doro-
thy is a saint, you hear me, a saint.*

(LIL' SMURF and BABY DEE drags SNOOKY out the apartment; KILO closes the door, turns around and looks at MILSAP)

KILO
Now it's time for you to bounce Sap.

MILSAP
(shuttering)
C'mon Kilo, I got sumthing to put on it.

KILO
How much ya got Sap.

MILSAP
(shuttering and going through his pockets)
How much I got, well, mane I got a toothbrush, 12 cent, some candy, and a pencil.

KILO
Is that all Milsap?

MILSAP
(shuttering)
Nall, wait one second.

(MILSAP takes his shoe off and then takes off his sock)

MILSAP
(shuttering)
How bout my lucky sock?

(KILO starts to hold his nose)

KILO
(holding his nose)
It's time to for you to leave kinfolk.

(KILO escorts MILSAP to the front door)

MILSAP
(shuttering and begging)
C'mon Kilo, don't kick me out, how you gone treat a brotha like this.

KILO
Easy

(KILO slams the door in MILSAP'S face and walks back to the couch and lay down; then someone knocks on the door)

KILO
(opens the door)
What do you want Milsap?

(KILO has to look twice because it wasn't MILSAP at the door, but a police officer named Buckley carrying a bag)

KILO
(grinning)
Well, isn't it good ole Officer Buckley.

BUCKLEY
What's up KILO

KILO
Nothing much, hey come on in, take a seat and holla at ya boy.

(BUCKLEY came in the apartment and they both walked toward couch; KILO takes out a blunt, blazes it up and starts smoking)

KILO
(smoking the blunt)
So, what can I do for you officer.

> BUCKLEY
> Cut the crap Kilo, you know what's I'm here for.

> KILO
> (smoking the blunt)
> Calm down Buckley, you seem a little uptight, just calm down.

> BUCKLEY
> I'm supposed to report back on duty in 10 minutes.

> KILO
> (smoking the blunt)
> Fo real, well let's get to it then.

(BUCKLEY puts the bag on the table, opens it and takes out a pound of kush)

> BUCKLEY
> Aight Kilo, this been in the police storage area for bout a month now.

> KILO
> Is that what I think it is.

> BUCKLEY
> A pound of kush, and it's quality too, not that cheap, imitating stuff they try and sell you on the streets.

> KILO
> I bet it is, let me hold that for a second.

(BUCKLEY gave KILO the pound of kush and KILO starts smelling it)

> KILO
> (smelling the kush)
> Mane, I love the smell of kush in the afternoon.

BUCKLEY
Now listen up Kilo, There's a lot more kush where that came from in this bag right here, it's was hard to get it but I did it, you sell this on the streets for a reasonable price, make that profit grown, break me off with my share and we got ourselves a deal here.

KILO
You know what, I like the sound of that kinfolk, and here my part of the deal.

(KILO reaches under the couch, takes out a suitcase and laid it on the table, he opens it and it was fills with money)

KILO
It looks like we both bout to get what we want, but next time, get me a hold of that cocaine cuz, I need that nose candy mane.

BUCKLEY
Yeah whateva.
(BUCKLEY closes the suitcase and gets up from the couch, then KILO puts his blunt out in the ashtray and gets up)

KILO
Wait a minute bra, what's wrong with you.

BUCKLEY
You know what, I kinda hate this Kilo, I have a wife and two kids, I'm a police officer for god sake and I'm stealing drugs for you.

KILO
Buckley, you knew what the deal was when you got in this, it's all bout that money fool, you're my silence partner in this operation, ain't nobody go find out, you makin' money, I'm makin' money, that's all that matters.

> *BUCKLEY*
> *Yeah, I guess you right, I'm bout to report back on duty, I guess I holla at ya later.*

> *KILO*
> *Aight fool.*

> *(KILO and BUCKLEY shook hands and BUCKLEY leaves; KILO laid back down on the couch; the music starts back playing in the background; he took his blunt out the ashtray, lights it back up and starts smoking)*

SCENE 7
BIGGS AND CALVIN

(Takes place at BRIANA'S house a month later, YVETTE PARKER is in the living room talking to DET. BIGGS, who came over to see CALVIN; Ms. Gloria enters the scene with a cup of coffee)

DET. BIGGS
Thank you Ma'am.

(DET BIGGS takes the coffee and MS. GLORIA sits down in her rocking chair)

YVETTE PARKER
So, tell me Detective, what kind of trouble is Calvin in this time.

MS. GLORIA
Don't start Yvette.

YVETTE PARKER
(smiling)
Now momma, it's not nice to interrupt, let the Detective speak.

DET. BIGGS
(drinking his coffee)
Don't worry Ma'am, Calvin isn't in trouble, He hasn't violated anything or started any trouble, to tell you the truth, I think he changed his ways.

MS. GLORIA
Listen to the Detective Yvette, I told you Calvin changed his ways, he's one of the nicest boys I've ever known Detective.

YVETTE PARKER
Well, if he isn't in trouble, then what are you doing here Detective.

DET. BIGGS
I'm just here to check up on him, to see how he's doing, discuss a few issues with him.

MS. GLORIA
All, he's doing fine Detective, he's just a well-mannered young man and a sweetheart.

YVETTE PARKER
Yeah, Yeah, Yeah, but what kind of issues are you talking about Detective.

MS. GLORIA
(talking to her daughter)
I don't think that's none of your business Yvette.

(Before DET. BIGGS could say anything else, someone knocks on the door)

YVETTE PARKER
(smiling)
Momma, can you get the door, I wanna discuss some things to the detective about Calvin.

(MS. GLORIA looks at her sneaky daughter and MS. GLORIA gets up from the couch and walks toward the door)

DET. BIGGS
(looking at his watch)
Well, you know, I should be going, I gotta go back on duty, maybe I catch up with Calvin next time.

YVETTE PARKER
Don't be silly Detective, it won't take long, they should be on their way back from church.

MS. GLORIA
Yeah, I would've went to church detective but I'm still sore.

DET. BIGGS
Sore, what wrong ma'am.

MS. GLORIA
The pastor child, he preach a sermon last night in the bedroom, Lord Have Mercy On My Soul, I swear that man knows a way with words detective.

DET. BIGGS
(grins)
I hear ya ma'am.

YVETTE PARKER
Ma, stop acting so freaky.

MS. GLORIA
Child I'm not freaky, just experience, all of this is experience.

(MS. GLORIA opens the door; BRIANA, CALVIN, and KEISHA came in)

MS. GLORIA
(yells)
CALVIN!!

YVETTE PARKER
(smiling)
CALVIN, well isn't this a surprise, come on it, Detective Biggs is here to see you.

(CALVIN *then looks at DET. BIGGS and he knew something was going on*)

KEISHA
Detective, what you do this time Calvin.

BRIANA
Will you shut up Keisha, he hasn't done anything, haven't you.

KEISHA
Of course he did something, the police here, what is it Calvin, you rob a bank, sold some crack, some rocks, that good dro, what is it.

BRIANA
Be quiet Keisha

CALVIN
(curious)
What's going on

DET BIGGS
Come and take a seat Calvin, there's something we need to discuss, if you ladies don't mind, can I talk to him alone.

YVETTE PARKER
Oh, we don't mind detective.

BRIANA
But I mind.

YVETTE PARKER
Briana

BRIANA
But momma…

(*Before BRIANA could say anything else, CALVIN cuts her off*)

CALVIN
Briana, it's okay.

*(CALVIN looks at BRIANA and gave her a kiss; then YVETTE
PARKER gets up from the couch)*

YVETTE PARKER
*Okay then, why don't we go out and eat at a restaurant, maybe
some Chinese food or something.*

MS. GLORIA
You mean I don't have to cook, I'll take that deal.

KEISHA
Bet, I'm hungry as hell.

YVETTE PARKER
What did you say Keisha?

KEISHA
I mean, I'm hungry as heck ma; let's head out.

*(KEISHA, MS. GLORIA, and YVETTE PARKER leaves out
the house)*

BRIANA
I'll bring you something back for the restaurant, ok baby.

CALVIN
Aight Briana.

*(BRIANA kisses Calvin, then she looks at DET. BIGGS and
leaves the house, Calvin then looks at BIGGS)*

DET. BIGGS
Come take a seat Calvin, relax, I won't bite, I already ate today.

(*Then BIGGS giggle for a minute, CALVIN still looks at BIGGS*)

DET. BIGGS
I'm just joking with ya Cal, come sit down.

(*CALVIN looks at DET. BIGGS again and he takes a seat on the couch*)

DET. BIGGS
(*smiling*)
What's up Calvin, what you been up too.

CALVIN
Nothing much, just working hard.

DET. BIGGS
All yeah, I hear you got a job at Pizza Hut delivering pizza, how you like it.

CALVIN
It's aight.

DET. BIGGS
Aight huh, well maybe one day you can hook me up with a large supreme, but judging my weight, food is the last thing I need, ain't that right.

(*DET. BIGGS just laughing at his comment and CALVIN just smiles a little, thinking to himself why is DET. BIGGS here at his girlfriend's house*)

DET. BIGGS
But me being real Calvin, I'm proud of ya, I see a lot of changes in ya, You staying out the streets, you living with some nice people, and you got a steady job, It may not bring in the money you use to having but it's a steady job.

Cecil Jarrell Dowden's DopeBoy Hustle - The Play

(CALVIN then looks at BIGGS)

CALVIN
*I appreciate that Biggs but enough with the small talk, why are
you really here.*

(BIGGS pauses for a second, and looks back at CALVIN)

DET. BIGGS
Well Calvin, Kashon Wilkins is the reason why I'm here.

CALVIN
(surprise)
You talking bout.

DET. BIGGS
Yeah, I'm talking about Kilo, he's out of jail.

CALVIN
All mane.

(Calvin pauses for a second)

CALVIN
It's been a year already.

DET. BIGGS
*I'm afraid so Cal, he got last month and since he been out, drugs
have been running through this neighborhood, there has even
been drugs stolen from police evidence.*

CALVIN
*Oh, well I don't know nothing about that Biggs, I haven't seen
Kilo, I didn't even know he was out.*

DET. BIGGS
Don't worry bout it Cal, I ain't trying to accuse you, I know

you livin' a better life now, I mean you not involved with drugs anymore, at least I hope.

(CALVIN looks at BIGGS and pauses)

DET. BIGGS
Well, aren't you, you know that against yo probation.

CALVIN
I ain't in the dope game anymore Biggs.

DET. BIGGS
That's good to hear, because if you are, you can seek help, there are a lot of programs that are drug related that you could partici-pate in, plus you could seek counseling.

CALVIN
Counseling and programs, you know I did that already Biggs and they say the same old thing, those people don't understand or know what I been through.

DET. BIGGS
I understand Calvin.

CALVIN
Yeah right.

DET. BIGGS
What, you thought that I was always a cop, mane when I was young, I use to be the biggest drug dealer on the block, nobody couldn't tell me nothing, I always use to stay into it with the police.

CALVIN
What made you change?

DET. BIGGS

I found God Calvin, he showed me the way out, I realize that I didn't need drugs in my life anymore because I have God, I want others to realize they don't need drugs either, that's why I became a cop, to serve and protect, listen, I know that you grew up on the wrong side of the tracks, being an orphan, you and Kashon raised at that terrible orphanage, not growing up in a stable environment, that's hard for a child, but I can tell you this, drugs aren't the answer, I see a lot of potential in ya Cal, too much potential, don't let it go to waste, don't let the streets corrupt you.

CALVIN

I know that already, I know drugs aren't the answer but what if that's all you know, what if that was all that you were taught, what if that is all you can live by.

DET. BIGGS

that sound like something the old Calvin would say.

CALVIN

Maybe there's still some of that old Calvin inside of me.

DET. BIGGS

Don't say that, I mean look, you got a good thing happening for you, you have a pregnant girlfriend, you got responsibilities now, don't throw that away. You got a second chance to make things right, don't mess that up.

CALVIN

I'll try.

DET. BIGGS

(yelling)
Don't try Calvin, do it, I'm saying this because I don't wanna see you behind bars.

CALVIN
(yelling back)
What you want me to do Biggs, huh, what you want me to do,
everyday I be struggling' mane, it gets harder and harder as each
day comes, I feel like life is kickin' my ass, you know.

DET. BIGGS
It'll be ok Cal, trust me on this, life is not easy, but you got to
know what's right from wrong, you got to struggle to find success,
that's part of life, but in the meantime, just stay away from Kilo,
I know he's your brother but he's nothing but trouble, alright.
Use your head Cal, don't get caught up with this dope because
there are too many young brothers like you in jail already.

(CALVIN puts his head down)

DET. BIGGS
Listen to me Calvin, aight.

CALVIN
Aight

DET. BIGGS
Hey Calvin.

(CALVIN looks at BIGGS)

DET. BIGGS
Take care of yourself mane.

(CALVIN shakes his head up and down and DET. BIGGS
leaves out the door)

SCENE 8
REALIZING THE STRUGGLE

*(Takes place later on that night over BRIANA'S HOUSE,
BRIANA is on the couch watching tv and sopping while eating
a carton of ice cream while the floor is filled with chip bags and
candy wrappers, then CALVIN enters the house in his Pizza Hut
uniform just getting off work)*

BRIANA
(sopping and eating ice cream)
Hey Baby.

(CALVIN walks toward BRIANA)

CALVIN
What's wrong bri, why you crying and what happen to the living
room, it looks like Katrina came back and hit this place.

BRIANA
(sopping and eating ice cream)
It's nothing, I'm just watching Good Times, this is the episode
they found out James died in that car accident, it always brings
me to tears.

CALVIN
All hell, I thought it was something really wrong with you.

(Exhausted CALVIN took a seat on the couch beside BRIANA)

BRIANA
You look worn out baby, you had a hard night at work.

CALVIN
(exhausted)
Hell yeah, I had to prep breadsticks, personal pans, large and medium hand toss, oil large and medium pans, fold boxes, cook, cut, waited a couple of tables, went on a couple of deliveries, then when we close, I had to take the garbage out, clean the bathrooms, parking lot, mop and sweep the floor, mane my shoulders is killin' me baby.

BRIANA
Po baby, let me give you a nice massage.

(BRIANA then gave CALVIN a massage, which was making CALVIN feeling real good)

CALVIN
(relaxing)
Dang girl, you know you got some magic fingers.

BRIANA
I know

CALVIN
I know too, and if you keep doing that, we gone have to go to the back and do you know what.

BRIANA
Yeah right Calvin

CALVIN
We might as well, you already pregnant so we don't have to sneak around and hide it from ya momma like we used too.

(BRIANA stop massaging CALVIN'S shoulders and gave him a love tap on the head)

BRIANA
Boy you crazy, and you making me missing my episode.

(BRIANA starts back watching tv)

BRIANA
If you hungry baby, I brought you some Chinese rice back from the restaurant, it's in the fridge.

CALVIN
(tired)
I appreciate that baby, but I might just hit the bed, I gotta work a double shift tomorrow.

BRIANA
Oh okay.

(When CALVIN got up from the couch, BRIANA grabs his hand)

BRIANA
Before you go to bed, can we talk for a minute?

CALVIN
(tired)
Aight, but make it quick baby, I'm too tired.

(CALVIN sits back down on the couch)

BRIANA
Listen Calvin, we been together for three years and we can tell each other anything right.

CALVIN
Yeah.

BRIANA
I hope there aren't any secrets between us because we don't need that.

CALVIN
What you trying to get at bay?

BRIANA
Ok Calvin, let me just stop beating around the bush, why was Detective Biggs here.

(CALVIN pauses for a second)

CALVIN
Why was he here?

BRIANA
Yeah, I didn't shutter, why Biggs was here, are you in any trouble, are you still smoking and selling drugs.

CALVIN
All here you go with that, nall girl he was just checking up on me, to see how I was doing that's all.

BRIANA
That's all

CALVIN
Yeah, that's all.

BRIANA
I hope so Calvin, I hope you're not lying to me.

CALVIN
BRIANA, look at me baby, I will never lie to you. Our relationship is too deep and too serious to hold secrets aight.

BRIANA
Ok Cal Ok, you made your point.

CALVIN

Now, since we got that straight, I'm tired baby, I been working all night, I only made four dollars tonight and my gas hand is damn near on empty so I bought to go to bed.

BRIANA

You only got four dollars.

CALVIN

Yeah.

(BRIANA looks at CALVIN and then took out her pocketbook)

CALVIN

(upset)

What you doing?

(BRIANA took a twenty dollar bill out her pocketbook and was trying to hand it to CALVIN)

BRIANA

(trying to hand CALVIN the money)

Here Calvin, here's a twenty, I know how high gas is.

CALVIN

(upset)

Briana, I don't want your money.

BRIANA

(trying to hand CALVIN the money)

Take it Calvin

CALVIN

(upset)

Nall Briana, I'm not used to too many handouts, I'm always used to having money in my pocket when I used to be a dope boy.

BRIANA
(trying to hand CALVIN the money)
Well, you're not a dope boy anymore, you're living a better life now, it's not about the money, It was never about the money, we're a couple and we bout to start a family, we need to support each other Calvin, not you trying to take care of everything.

CALVIN
(upset)
Yeah, Yeah, Yeah,

BRIANA
Take it Calvin or I'm just gone put it in your car when I drive it, anyway it goes, this twenty's going in the car so stop being so damn cocky and take the money.

(CALVIN looks at BRIANA with an upset look on his face and takes the money)

BRIANA
Now, since I made that clear, I'm bought to go to bed.

(BRIANA gets up from the couch and starts whining, CALVIN is still sitting on the couch, then BRIANA stops walking)

BRIANA
Are you coming to lay with me for a while before you go in your room and go to sleep.

CALVIN
(upset)
Nall, I decided I'm just gonna stay up for a minute.

BRIANA
Suit yourself.

(BRIANA leaves while CALVIN is on the couch thinking)

SCENE 9
CALVIN LOVES MARY JANE

(Takes place a week later at BRIANA'S house; CALVIN is laid on the couch sleep; then BRIANA and KEISHA comes in)

BRIANA
Hey Calvin baby, we bout to walk to the park, you wanna come.

(Then BRIANA and KEISHA notice that CALVIN is sleep on the couch)

KEISHA
I think your boy is sleep sis.

BRIANA
I see.

(BRIANA grabs a blanket that was laid across and chair, proceeds to walk toward CALVIN on the couch and covers his body up with the blanket)

KEISHA
What's wrong with Calvin, he been sitting on the couch watching tv and sleep for the past week, he needs to get his lazy behind up and come walk with us.

(BRIANA sits on the couch beside CALVIN)

BRIANA
(rubbing his head)

He's just exhausted that's all, working all day and night, double shifts back to back, po baby.

KEISHA
Mane, forget dude, let's go to the park and check out dis boys playing basketball with their shirts off sweating and looking good, come on Bri before I miss that.

BRIANA
I might just stay here with him Keisha, look how cute he is just sleeping.

KEISHA
Come on girl, you spend time with him all the time and never have time for me, we sisters and we need to bond more, you know.

BRIANA
Ok, let me just look at him for a few more seconds.

KEISHA
Come on BRIANA, we wasting quality time.

(BRIANA looks back at her sister who was standing by the doorway, then she looks back at CALVIN, kisses him on the cheek and walk towards the doorway)

(BRIANA proceeds to walks toward KEISHA who was standing by the doorway; then they both leave; A few seconds past and CALVIN is still sleep on the couch, he starts tossing, turning, and talking to himself in his sleep while on the couch because he is having a nightmare about KILO; then he accidentally falls off the couch and wakes up on the floor)

CALVIN
(talking to himself)
Just relax Calvin, it was just a dream, you don't have anything to worry about, just relax, you can handle this, I just need to clear my mind that's all.

(CALVIN gets up from the floor and then sits back on the couch)

CALVIN
Mane, I need to hit a blunt, hey Briana, Keisha, Yvette Parker, Ms. Gloria

(CALVIN didn't hear anything in the house)

CALVIN
I guess nobody's here.

(CALVIN takes out a blunt and a lighter, blazes it up and took one long hit)

CALVIN
(after the first hit)
That's all you needed Calvin, mane I feel a little better now.

(CALVIN takes a couple of more hits; then he started hearing a sweet voice calling his name)

MARY JANE
(voice)
Calvin

CALVIN
(sitting on the couch)
Who said that; BRIANA?

(CALVIN didn't hear anything else, so he didn't pay it any attention so he starts back smoking, then he hears the voice again)

MARY JANE
(voice)
CALVIN

CALVIN
(paranoid)

What's who's calling my name.

MARY JANE
(voice)
CALVIN.

(CALVIN, paranoid as ever, gets up from the couch)

CALVIN
(looking at the blunt)
Mane, I must be high as hell.

MARY JANE
(voice)
Calvin

CALVIN
(talking to himself)
Hey cuz, stop playing games now, who's calling my name, what is it that you want.

MARY JANE
(voice)
I want you Calvin.

CALVIN
(paranoid)
Say what.

(A cloud of smoke appears and a beautiful girl dressed in white walks toward CALVIN; Stunned by her beauty, CALVIN was just looking)

MARY JANE
Hey Calvin

CALVIN
(stunned)
Heeeey!

(Then MARY JANE and CALVIN start smiling)

CALVIN
Excuse me for asking this but who are you and why are you here.

MARY JANE
I'm the girl of your dreams Calvin.

CALVIN
Fo' real, the girl of my dreams

(CALVIN looks up to the sky and said thank you lord and then
looks back at MARY JANE)

CALVIN
(smiling)
So, you're the girl of my dreams

MARY JANE
Yes Calvin, every time you smoke

(CALVIN then looks at the blunt in his hand, then he looks
back at the girl)

CALVIN
Mary Jane

MARY JANE
Yes Calvin, and I'm here because I want to be with you, forever.

(MARY JANE tries to move closer to CALVIN moves back)

CALVIN
Wait a minute, Just wait a minute, hold on cuz I don't under-
stand what the hell is going on, I must be high fo real.

(CALVIN then puts the blunt out in the ashtray; MARY JANE
watched as he did it)

MARY JANE
See Calvin, how can you treat weed like that; you need me.

CALVIN
Stop Mary Jane.

MARY JANE
What is it, it's Briana isn't it.

CALVIN
I'm in love with her.

MARY JANE
I remember it was a point in time when you was in love with
me, don't let Briana come between what we shared.

CALVIN
I know Mary Jane, but I care about her, a lot.

MARY JANE
You can't let me go Calvin, I can see it in your eyes.

(CALVIN looks at MARY JANE and then closes his eyes)

CALVIN
(eyes close shaking his head)
Just leave Mary Jane

MARY JANE
You can't get me out your mind, can you, it's just a matter of
time that Briana finds out about us.

CALVIN
(shaking his head)
Nall, Nall

MARY JANE
Calvin, listen sweetie, you gotta choose; it's either me or her, it
can't be both.

(CALVIN looks at MARY JANE for a few seconds, thinking that
he really lost his mind and went crazy, but finally realize what
was more important to him)

CALVIN
Then I choose Briana

MARY JANE
Listen to what you are saying.

CALVIN
I know what I'm saying, I realize that you are nothing but
trouble, an evil addiction and that Briana Chantel Parker is the
only girl I'm addicted too, now that it's all said and done, you
can bounce.

(MARY JANE looks at CALVIN for a minute)

MARY JANE
Ok Calvin, so I guess this is good-bye

CALVIN
Goodbye Mary J, we had a long run but I don't need you, I have
Briana and that's all I need.

(CALVIN watches as MARY JANE disappears in the smoke,
then CALVIN just stood there, in front of the couch, for a couple
of seconds thinking about MARY JANE)

SCENE 10
BRIANA'S DILEMMA

(Takes place on a corner; BABY DEE and LIL' SMURF are shooting dice while SNOOKY is laid back on the wall smoking)

LIL' SMURF
(talking trash to DEE)
You can't beat me Dee, I'm telling ya, this game is mine.

BABY DEE
Whateva Smurf, just keep rollin'

LIL' SMURF
Aight then; Come on lucky seven.

(LIL' SMURF rolls the dice and hit a seven on his roll)

LIL' SMURF
(excited)
Lucky seven, I told you Dee, now gimme my mon-nee.

(LIL SMURF takes the money that he won and he was so happy that he started doing his happy dance; then MILSAP comes walking around and interrupts BABY DEE and LIL' SMURF)

MILSAP
(talking to LIL' SMURF, shuttering)
Hey mane, can I borrow two dollas.

LIL' SMURF
(counting his money)
Two dollars, for what.

MILSAP
(shuttering)
Yeah mane, I need sumthing to eat mane.

LIL' SMURF
Hey Sap, look at my face mane, do it look like I give a damn.

MILSAP
(looking at SMURF'S face)
I don't know

LIL' SMURF
Get on down Sap, you smell like a wet dog too, get the hell on.

(BABY DEE and LIL' SMURF start laughing and joking on MILSAP; then MILSAP sneaks and takes some money from LIL' SMURF'S hand and tries to run away but BABY DEE caught him and two starts kicking and hitting MILSAP)

SNOOKY
(laid back on the wall smoking)
Smurf and Dee, leave that crackhead alone, he ain't worth ya'll time.

(After SNOOKY said that, BABY DEE and LIL' SMURF stops hitting and kicking MILSAP)

BABY DEE
You lucky this time Sap; Now get outta here.

LIL' SMURF
And don't let us catch you around here either.

(MILSAP gets up and runs off; LIL' SMURF starts picking up his money and BABY DEE helps him; then BRIANA and KEISHA starts walking toward their way talking; when they saw SNOOKY, they stopped walking and looked at the guys)

SNOOKY
Yess saa, look who it is ya'll, the Parker sisters, let's have a little fun shall we.

(SNOOKY, BABY DEE, and LIL' SMURF walks toward the girls; SNOOKY starts to check BRIANA out while BABY DEE and LIL' SMURF stands behind SNOOKY and look)

SNOOKY
(checking BRIANA out)
Well, Well, Well, Briana Parker, even when she's pregnant she's still the finest girl on the block, girl you so fine I'll drink your bath water I swear the God I will.

BRIANA
What is it that you want Stacey?

SNOOKY
Please, call me Snooky, I just wanna holla at cha for a minute, is that too much, I mean, I was your first you know, and then after we broke up, you started going with my boy Calvin but it's all good though.

BRIANA
What the hell you talking bout Stacey?

SNOOKY
(checking BRIANA out)
You know exactly what I'm talking about, you know what we had was special?

BRIANA
What was special bout is Stacey, you were my baby sister, you took me to McDonald's, and besides we didn't even eat inside, we went through the drive thru, that what you call special.

SNOOKY
All, it's like that now huh, I bet you wasn't complaining when you got your meal supersize.

BRIANA
Boy it been like that, you are pitiful Stacey, 30 years old still staying at home with yo momma.

(BABY DEE and LIL' SMURF start laughing)

BABY DEE
Dang cuz, she dogged you out mane.

SNOOKY
I'm 28 years old and forget ya'll boys, it's only temporary ok, temporary, I'm gone move out my momma house, it's just taking a little time that all.

KEISHA
(talking to SNOOKY)
Whateva Stacey, but if you can excuse us guys, we gotta be on our way, okay.

(BRIANA and KEISHA walked pass SNOOKY, BABY DEE, and LIL' SMURF and when they were about to walk around the corner, they heard Kilo's voice behind them)

KILO
(voice)
Why you girls leaving so soon?

(BRIANA and KEISHA stop; then they turned around and saw KILO; the girls were shock to see him, especially KEISHA; then KILO walks toward the girls)

KILO
(holding KEISHA'S hand)
What's up ladies?

(KILO kisses KEISHA on her hand and she looks like she wants to pass out)

KEISHA
(smiling)
Hey Kilo, long time no see.

(KILO and KEISHA start giving each other the eye and then BRIANA interrupted)

BRIANA
(talking to KILO)
What you doing here Kilo, you suppose to be in jail.

KILO
(smiling)
I'm out, I been out for bout a month now, what, you ain't glad to see me.

BRIANA
Hell nall

KILO
(smiling)
C'mon Briana, Don't break my heart like that.

(KILO then looks back at SNOOKY, BABY DEE, and LIL' SMURF and the four of them starts grinning; then he turns back toward BRIANA)

KILO
So Briana, I see your stomach got a little bigger since the last time I saw you.

BRIANA
I'm pregnant Kilo.

KILO
(acting like he's shocked)
Fo' real, and old boy Calvin is the daddy isn't he, a matter of
fact, where kinfolk at anyway, we have some catching up to do

BRIANA
(angry)
None of your damn business.

KILO
Uh Oh, feisty isn't she guys.

SNOOKY
Sho' is Kilo, that's what I like about her.

(BABY DEE and LIL' SMURF start grinning)

KILO
Well guys, I already made that deal so I think we should be going
now.

BRIANA
I see you still selling, how sad.

(KILO looks at BRIANA and starts smiling)

KILO
You know it and tell ya boy I said what's up and that he needs to
holla at me.

BRIANA
(angry)
Don't bet on it?

> KILO
> (smiling)
> Aight then, I see how it is, I'll holla at ya, let's go guys, see ya
> Keisha.

> KEISHA
> (smiling)
> Bye Kilo.

(KEISHA kept smiling at KILO until he left with the guys; then
KEISHA was in a trance)

> BRIANA
> (shock)
> I can't believe this Keisha, can you.

(BRIANA saw that her sister was in a trance and tries to snap
her out)

> BRIANA
> (snapping her fingers at KEISHA)
> KEISHA, KEISHA

(KEISHA snaps out the trance)

> KEISHA
> Huh, what.

> BRIANA
> I know that look Keisha and don't even think about it, Kilo is
> not your type.

> KEISHA
> What you talking about, I just think he's cute that's all.

BRIANA
Well, think something else, we better head back to the house so I can tell Calvin that Kilo is out.

(BRIANA was about to turn around but KEISHA stops her)

KEISHA
Wait a minute sis, I thought we were going to the park remember, don't even worry about Kilo.

BRIANA
I don't know, what if he comes looking for Calvin.

KEISHA
Don't worry so much, Calvin will be aight, so let's go already.

BRIANA
Aight Keisha, let's go.

(BRIANA and KEISHA leave)

SCENE 11
SURPRISE VISIT

*(Takes place a couple of hours later of BRIANA'S house; CAL-
VIN is holding a blunt in his hand talking to it)*

CALVIN
(holding the blunt; whining)
*I can't believe it's over between us, That I finally realize that I
don't need you anymore; that being with BRIANA is the only
thing I need and the only thing I want, but I ain't gone lie, we
had our good times though, you was always there when I needed
you, but I gotta make this move, I hope you understand.*

*(Suddenly someone knocks on the door; CALVIN quickly puts
the blunt back in the ashtray)*

CALVIN
Who is it?

MILSAP
(shuttering)
It's Milsap

CALVIN
Oh hell, I wonder what he wants.

*(CALVIN gets up from the couch and walks toward the door,
opens the door and it was Milsap, standing there looking like a
junkie)*

MILSAP
(shuttering)

What's up Calvin, mane it's good to see ya?

(MILSAP picks up CALVIN and starts squeezing him)

CALVIN
What's up Sap, you can put me down now, you squeezing a little too tight cuz.

MILSAP
(shuttering)
Oh, my bad cuz.

(MILSAP then puts CALVIN down)

CALVIN
What you want Milsap?

MILSAP
(shuttering)
What I want, mane I just came to see ya, see what ya been up too.

CALVIN
Don't play Sap, if you're here looking for some crack or some dope, you can go somewhere else, you know I don't sell drugs anymore cuz.

MILSAP
(shuttering)
C'mon Cal, you know me betta than that mane; I don't want no drugs.

CALVIN
Then what are you doing here.

MILSAP
(rubbing his stomach)
Mane, I'm so hungry cuz, can I borrow at least two dollas mane
so I can buy me a ham sandwich or sumthing to snack on.

(CALVIN looks at MILSAP and he felt a little sorry for him so
he went into his pocket and takes out a twenty dollar bill and
gives it to him)

CALVIN
Ok Sap, here's a twenty, buy some mouthwash and a bar of soap
while you at it.

(MILSAP looks at the twenty dollar bill)

MILSAP
(shuttering)
Twenty dolla, mane this a whole lotta money, thank Calvin.

CALVIN
Don't mention it and don't buy no drugs with that money either
Milsap, listen I want you to make good use of this money, I want
you to live a new life, starting with this twenty dollar bill, aight.

MILSAP
(shuttering, holding the twenty dollar bill)
Aight Calvin.

CALVIN
Aight, now it's time for you to bounce cuz.

(CALVIN opens the door and MILSAP proceeds to walk out)

CALVIN
Hey Sap.

MILSAP
(shuttering)
Yeah

CALVIN
Take care of yourself mane.

MILSAP
(shuttering)
I will, I will.

(MILSAP then walks out the door and CALVIN went back to the couch and laid back for a while and watches tv; A few seconds later, somebody else knocks on the door)

CALVIN
(talking to himself)
It must be Milsap again.

(CALVIN gets up from the couch and walks toward the door)

CALVIN
(opens the door)
What is it Sap?

(CALVIN was shock to find out that it wasn't MILSAP at the door, but it was KILO)

KILO
Calvin Dajuan Wilkins; holla at cha boy.

(KILO walks pass CALVIN and into the house; CALVIN then closes the door)

KILO
Mane, this is a nice house you living in kinfolk, far better than that orphanage that we both were raise at.

CALVIN
Yeah, it's a nice house aight.

(KILO then walks toward the couch, takes out a blunt, lights it up and starts smoking; CALVIN walks and stands beside the couch)

KILO
(smoking the blunt)
Mane, prison life was hard cuz, always looking over my shoulders worrying bout what these niggas would try and do to you, but I manage you know.

CALVIN
I know you did.

KILO
(smoking the blunt)
So, tell me about you Cal, what you been doing this past year.

(CALVIN then takes a seat beside KILO)

CALVIN
Well, you know after the drug bust we were in, I had to go to trial, Ms. Parker was my lawyer so she had it so they would send me to military boot camp instead of getting a year like you did at juve, so I went to boot camp for six months, it was hard dude, after that I came back home staying with my girl Briana, end up getting her pregnant and now I'm working at Pizza Hut as a delivery driver.

KILO
(smoking the blunt)
Dawg Calvin, that's quite a story mane, but you know I heard a different story.

CALVIN
What you hear?

(KILO puts the blunt out in the ashtray)

KILO
Well, I heard that one of the biggest drug carriers on the block sold out.

(CALVIN stands up)

CALVIN
(standing up)
So you saying I sold out.

KILO
I ain't saying nothing cuz, I'm just telling you what I heard.

CALVIN
I don't need to sell drugs no more Kilo and what you saying bout I sold out is a bunch of bull, I just grew up that's all.

(KILO stands up from the couch)

KILO
Look at what you saying, The old Calvin would never say anything like that.

CALVIN
Well, the old Calvin is dead kinfolk, I got responsibilities now cuz, a second chance at things, and it was time for a change.

KILO
Listen to me Cal, I'm your brother, Dopeboys for life remember, we grew up in the same neighborhood together, we both orphans mane, our mom even sold dope.

CALVIN
Yeah she did and she got hook on heroin too and overdose.

KILO
Nigga I know, I remember that night just like it was yesterday, She was sitting at the table with the needle in her arm, I seen her eyes roll behind her head bruh, I seen her body fall to the floor, looking at her lifeless body just laying there, I was only 5 bruh and you was 4 but you was sleep but I seen it with my own eyes.

CALVIN
Then we need to end this cycle bruh, mom died in this dope game so that gotta tell you something, even though mom is dead, I feel like my brother is dead too, just give it up bruh, just give up the dope game Kashon.

(When CALVIN said his real name, KILO got mad)

KILO
(angry)
Don't call me Kashon, it's Kilo alright, don't you ever call me by that name again.

CALVIN
(talking back)
Or what Kashon, what you gone do about it.

(KILO and CALVIN just look at each other for a few seconds)

KILO
DopeBoys for life Calvin, that's how it was, that's how it was suppose to be, but I guess things change over this past year.

CALVIN
I guess it did.

KILO

I hate to hear that folk, like I said you are my brother Cal, I'm out here selling this dope making the money on my own, I'm ridin' a Crown Vic sittin on dem 26's by selling pounds of kush and some coke in only one month; hustling 24/7, don't have time to sleep kinfolk., too busy making money, and what are you doing, working at Pizza Hut as a damn delivery driver making tips in a busted down blazer; well here is my tips kinfolk.

(KILO takes out a roll of money; Calvin stares at it)

KILO
(holding the money)
Don't that look nice cuz; you can be makin' this; makin' real money; and if you decide you wanna make real money; holla at me at the Blue Revenue, Apartment 33, so we can get back on this hustle bruh; like we used too, I'm out cuz I gotta make this money.

(KILO looks at CALVIN and he turns around and walks toward the door; KILO stops at the door and looks back at CALVIN and he looks back at KILO; then KILO opens the door and walks out)

(After seeing KILO walks out, CALVIN takes a seat back on the couch and put his hands over his eyes; a few seconds passed, then BRIANA and KEISHA come in the house)

BRIANA
(yelling)
Hey Calvin, there's something I have to tell you.

(Then BRIANA and KEISHA start sniffing their noses)

KEISHA
Hey, it smells like someone been smoking.

(BRIANA and KEISHA look at the blunt that was put on in the ashtray)

KEISHA
(smiling)
Someone has been smoking.

(BRIANA looks at CALVIN and CALVIN gets up from the couch; BRIANA walks toward CALVIN)

CALVIN
It's not what it looks like Bri.

BRIANA
(angry)
Well, what does it look like Calvin.

KEISHA
(joking)
Uh Oh, you got busted.

CALVIN
Just let me explain bay.

BRIANA
(crossing her arms)
Explain yourself.

CALVIN
Ok, this might sound a little strange.

BRIANA
(crossed her arms)
I'm listening.

(KEISHA stands next to her sister and crosses her arms)

KEISHA
(crossed her arms)
Nall, we're listening.

CALVIN
Ok, I was smoking at first, but then I got a visit from Mary Jane, you know marijuana, and I was listening to all the things she was saying and she made me realize how much I love you Bri and that I don't need drugs in my life, after that, Kilo came over and that his blunt right there he was smoking, and we talked for a few minutes and he left.

(BRIANA and KEISHA look at CALVIN with their arms still cross)

KEISHA
What the hell you been smoking Calvin, whatever it was it had to be good for you to come up with a story like that.

CALVIN
Please stay outta this Keisha.

(CALVIN then grabs BRIANA'S hand)

CALVIN
C'mon Bri, I wouldn't lie to you girl, you gotta believe me.

(BRIANA looks at CALVIN with an upset look on her face and then she turns to her sister)

KEISHA
Don't believe him girl, he trying to play you like a fool.

BRIANA
(upset)
Keisha, can you leave me and Calvin along for a second and get rid of that blunt before momma and grandma get home.

KEISHA
Why I gotta leave when things get interesting?

> BRIANA
> *(upset)*
> *Please Keisha.*

> KEISHA
> *Ok Ok*

(KEISHA takes the ashtray off the table)

> KEISHA
> *You know what, I never like you anyway Calvin*

(KEISHA rolls her eyes at CALVIN and leaves)

> CALVIN
> *(talking to BRIANA)*
> *C'mon Bri, you gotta talk to me.*

(BRIANA still didn't say anything)

> CALVIN
> *(talking to BRIANA)*
> *C'mon Briana, don't be mad at me now.*

(BRIANA sits down on the couch and didn't say anything and this made CALVIN really frustrated; then CALVIN sits down on the couch)

> CALVIN
> *(talking to BRIANA)*
> *Aight then, if you go act like that, I guess we just go sit here all day on this couch and don't say anything to each other.*

(CALVIN and BRIANA sat on the couch for a couple of seconds, then finally BRIANA had something to say)

BRIANA
Calvin, why did you lie to me, I thought you said you stop smoking.

CALVN
I'm sorry bay, I didn't mean to lie to you, it was just something I found hard to talk to you about.

(BRIANA starts yelling at CALVIN)

BRIANA
(yelling)
Hard to talk to me about, I'm pregnant with your child Calvin and you have a serious drug problem.

CALVIN
I promise to you Briana that I'm given up smoking.

BRIANA
(yelling)
Whateva, why should I believe you and you lied to me the first time around. Maybe I should make you an appointment to go see that drug counselor, Mr. Turner.

CALVIN
I don't need counseling Bri, so I smoke a couple of blunts every day, I still take care of you, I mean, I do have a job at Pizza Hut.

BRIANA
(yelling)
A delivery driver Calvin, how the hell you think that job can support us, you be better off working at McDonald's; at least our child could get a free happy meal.

CALVIN
(yelling back)

All it's like that huh Bri, well maybe I should leave.

(CALVIN gets up from the couch)

BRIANA
All nall negro, you ain't going nowhere.

(BRIANA grabs CALVIN'S arm)

CALVIN
Girl, you better let me go.

BRIANA
(pulling CALVIN'S arm)
You ain't going nowhere Calvin.

CALVIN
Bri, you better get your damn hands of me.

BRIANA
(pulling CALVIN'S arm)
Or what Calvin, you gone hit me, I know you ain't crazy.

CALVIN
Let go of me Bri.

BRIANA
(pulling CALVIN'S arm)
Or what Calvin, what

(CALVIN turns around and slaps BRIANA; then CALVIN starts yelling at her while she was holding her jaw and crying)

BRIANA
(holding her jaw crying)
I can't believe you hit me Calvin.

CALVIN
(yelling)
You made me do it Bri, I just can't take this anymore, I tried to
be a good man to you, I gave up selling dope for you, I got this
stupid ass job at Pizza Hut working with people I don't even like
because of you, I changed my ways because of you and you don't
appreciate nothing I sacrificed. You know what, you can take
care of that baby by yourself cuz I'm going back on the streets to
make some real money.

(CALVIN walks out and slams the door while BRIANA was
walking behind him; She starts crying heavily against the door
and then starts leaning down on the floor; then KEISHA comes
in the room)

KEISHA
(concern)
Bri, what's wrong with you, what happen.

BRIANA
(crying and yelling against the door)
He's gone, Calvin left me.

KEISHA
(concern)
Come on girl, let me help you to the couch.

(KEISHA helps BRIANA to the couch and BRIANA kept crying; she laid her head against her sister's shoulder)

KEISHA
(holding BRIANA)
Don't worry Bri, it will be aight, don't worry.

(BRIANA kept crying on her sister's shoulder)

101

SCENE 12
BUCKLEY'S CONFESSION

(Takes place at the police station; BIGGS and RAMIREZ are in the confession room waiting for BUCKLEY to come in)

BIGGS
Ok Ramirez, this is what we gone do, I'll be the good cop, you be the bad.

RAMIREZ
Why I always have to be bad?

BIGGS
Cuz you good at it, that's why.

RAMIREZ
You know, my ex-boyfriend said the same thing after I keyed his Mercedes and burned down his house.

BIGGS
You did what.

RAMIREZ
That's a whole nutta story.

BIGGS
I don't even wanna know bout it.

(Then BUCKLEY comes in the room handcuffed and he sits down in the chair that is located in the middle of the room)

BIGGS
What's up Buckley?

BUCKLEY
(scared)
Hey Biggs.

BIGGS
Don't look so scared Buck, we ain't gone hurt ya, we just need to ask you a few questions that's all, give us some simple answers and you can be on your way, ok.

BUCKLEY
(scared)
Ok

BIGGS
Proceed Ramirez

(Sexy Officer RAMIREZ walks slowly toward BUCKLEY with a grin on her face, then she suddenly snaps and grabs BUCKLEY by the shirt)

RAMIREZ
(yelling, grabs BUCKLEY by the shirt)
Ok Buck, what the hell you doing with pounds of dro in your locker.

BUCKLEY
(scared as hell)
Say What

RAMIREZ
(yelling, grabs BUCKLEY by the shirt)
What

*(RAMIREZ then starts slapping BUCKLEY across the head
numerous of times, then she stops)*

RAMIREZ
Now, tell me what I wanna know Buck.

BUCKLEY
(scared)
What the hell is wrong with you girl?

RAMIREZ
That's not the answer I'm looking for.

*(RAMIREZ then starts back slapping BUCKLEY across the
head a couple more times, then she stops)*

BUCKLEY
(scared)
*Stop it Ramirez ok, I don't know nothing bout no dro, aight,
now can you let me go, I gotta go to the bathroom.*

RAMIREZ
*You ain't going nowhere and since I can't get nothing from ya,
maybe my friend can get some answers outta ya.*

*(RAMIREZ then pulls out her gun; BUCKLEY gets really
scared)*

BIGGS
(singing)
She pulls out the beretta.

BUCKLEY
(scared as hell)
C'mon now Ramirez, it ain't that serious

RAMIREZ
(holding the gun)
You betta tell me something Buck, I'm a loose cannon, I have no patience.

BIGGS
I don't think she's playing Buckley, you know how crazy these females can be.

RAMIREZ
(looking at Biggs)
What you say Biggs?

BIGGS
Nothing, I'm gone stay outta this.

BUCKLEY
(scared as hell, crying)
Aight, the dro is for Kilo ok, I was stealing drugs for him to sell on the streets and he was breakin' me off with half, just please let me go.

(RAMIREZ slowly puts her gun away)

RAMIREZ
It seems like we got our man Biggs.

BIGGS
Yeah, I ain't surprise either, let's go get this fool but what the hell is that smell.

(BIGGS and RAMIREZ starts sniffing their noses trying to figure out what that odor was then they looked at BUCKLEY)

BUCKLEY
(scared)
I told ya I had to go to the bathroom.

BIGGS
Oh hell nall, let's go Ramirez.

BUCKLEY
(scared)
Yall just gone leave me here

RAMIREZ
I ain't coming near ya Buck, smelling like two wet dogs and a
dead skunk.

(BIGGS and RAMIREZ leaves the room)

BUCKLEY
(yelling)
How yall go leave me here, this is so messed up, C'mon Biggs,
Ramirez

(BUCKLEY then starts sniffing himself)

BUCKLEY
(yelling)
Damn, I smell bad, that's must be that burrito I ate earlier,
C'mon, somebody help me.

(BUCKLEY continues to yell for help)

SCENE 13
THE DRUG BUST II

(Takes place at KILO'S apartment later on that night; The music is blasting real loud; KILO is laid back on the couch talking to SNOOKY while he is smoking a blunt; BABY DEE and LIL' SMURF are on the floor shooting dice; a couple of seconds later, someone knocks on the door)

(KILO gets up from the couch)

KILO
(whispering)
Hey ya'll, cut that music down, somebody knockin' on the door.

(The music went down and KILO walks toward the door)

KILO
Who is it?

CALVIN
It's Calvin.

SNOOKY
(sitting in his chair)
Who

CALVIN
(yelled)
Calvin!

(KILO opens the door and it was CALVIN)

> KILO
> (extended his hand)
> What's up Cal?

> CALVIN
> What's up Kilo

(KILO and CALVIN did their handshake)

> KILO
> Come on in and take a seat.

(CALVIN said whats up to the other guys and and takes a seat
on the couch beside KILO)

> KILO
> After what you said to me earlier today, I wasn't expecting to see
> you again.

> CALVIN
> (upset)
> Yeah, I wasn't expecting to come over here either.

> KILO
> But you know, you're always welcome here, my crib is yo crib
> cuz.

> CALVIN
> (upset)
> Yeah.

(KILO saw how upset CALVIN looks)

> KILO
> Hey mane, what's wrong with you, you seem a little upset.

CALVIN
(upset)
I am mane, Briana's trippin about this baby and me doing drugs
and I just can't take it anymore, We just got in a huge argu-
ment and things got out of hand and I don't think I can ever
go back, her family never really like me, except for Ms. Gloria,
and I messed that up, I don't know what to do and I didn't have
anywhere else to go so I came here.

KILO
That's deep cuz, I told you that you need to get back on this dope
game cuz.

CALVIN
I believe I need to dawg, working at Pizza Hut just ain't gone do
it cuz.

KILO
Hell nall it ain't Cal, you need to make some real money and I
will help you cuz we are family mane, we look out for each other,
ain't that right guys.

(BABY DEE and LIL' SMURF said yeah and kept on shooting dice; KILO then looks at SNOOKY who is still smoking the
blunt and is high as hell)

KILO
Hey Snook, let Cal hit on that blunt mane, he has problems.

(SNOOKY stops smoking at looks at KILO)

SNOOKY
(high)
Noo saa, he didn't put in on this mane.

KILO

Hell, you ain't either, that's my kush that you are smoking for free.

SNOOKY
(high)
Sho' is, here you go mane.

(SNOOKY passes the blunt to KILO; KILO takes out his lighter, blazes it up and starts smoking it)

KILO
(smoking the blunt)
See Calvin, this is some good kush kinfolk, and it's making me a lot of money in the process too, Hey Smurf and Dee, stop what you doing for a minute and come hit this.

(LIL' SMURF and BABY DEE stop shooting dice and walks toward KILO; LIL' SMURF smokes it first and passes it to BABY DEE and he takes a long hit and was geeked out and he passes it back to SNOOKY)

SNOOKY
(looking at BABY DEE; still high)
Hey Dee, who you think you are, me ain't it.

(SNOOKY takes a couple of more hits from the blunt)

SNOOKY
(high)
Here you go Calvin.

(SNOOKY passes the blunt to CALVIN and CALVIN just looks at it)

CALVIN
(looking at the blunt)
Mane, I don't know, I'm trying to quit.

SNOOKY
(high)
Just one hit, it's calling your name cuz, it's saying smoke me Calvin, smoke me till I'm gone, damn I'm high as hell.

(CALVIN takes the blunt from SNOOKY)

KILO
Yeah my boy, just like the good ole days, remember when we used to just chill, smoke, get on these hoes and get this money kinfolk. Forget Briana, she's ain't nothing, girls come a dime a dozen, I wouldn't tell ya nothing wrong Cal, I miss you mane and I want you to get back on this dope boy hustle with me. All you gotta do is take a hit from the blunt and all your problems will disappear, just like smoke.

(KILO, SNOOKY, BABY DEE, and LIL' SMURF kept on pressuring CALVIN to smoke the blunt; CALVIN looks at his friends, then he looks back at the blunt and then he stands up)

CALVIN
(looking at the blunt)
Nall, I can't do this anymore.

KILO
What you talking bout Calvin?

(CALVIN drops the blunt on the floor and steps on it; the guys thought CALVIN was crazy for what he did)

KILO
(yelling)
What the hell you do that for, you ruin good weed mane.

CALVIN
(talking to the guys)
Listen up ya'll, I can't do this kinfolk, just look at us lo, we can do better than this, shooting dice, selling dope, and smoking' weed all day is not what I wanna be doing for the rest of my life.

KILO
Then what you wanna do Cal, work at Pizza Hut for the rest of your life then.

CALVIN
(talking to the guys)
Nall, I have dreams that I wanna achieve you know, maybe go back to school, try and get my GED, make something out my life, just like you guys should do, you know I'm bout to straighten my life up, I can't be doing this anymore, I'm going home to my girl cuz she needs me.

(KILO, SNOOKY, BABY DEE, and LIL' SMURF joked on CALVIN and he walks away from them and toward the door; When CALVIN got closer to the door; someone banged on the door)

DET. BIGGS
(yelled)
Open up, it's the police, this is a drug bust.

The Guys
DAMN!!!

(DET. BIGGS busted the door down; RAMIREZ aimed her gun at BABY DEE and LIL' SMURF while DET. BIGGS aimed his at KILO and CALVIN. They made the guys get on the floor then handcuffed them and took them through the door; SNOOKY is still sitting in chair still high and in a dazed; a few seconds later, BIGGS came back through the door and walks toward SNOOKY)

BIGGS
(talking to SNOOKY)
Aight Snooky, get yo big ass up too.

SNOOKY
(high as hell)

(SNOOKY gets up out the couch and tries to walks but is to high and he falls a couple of time before being escorted by BIGGS out the apartment)

SCENE 14
BREAKIN' NEWS

(Takes place over BRIANA'S house; BRIANA is crying on MS. GLORIA's shoulder while YVETTE PARKER is walking in paces and KEISHA is sitting in the chair)

MS. GLORIA
(holding BRIANA)
Don't worry Briana, it'll be alright.

BRIANA
(crying)
Calvin left me grandma and he ain't coming back.

MS. GLORIA
(holding BRIANA)
Just don't worry about it baby.

YVETTE PARKER
(angry)
I can't believe what that boy did, I swear to god I'm gone kill him the next time I see him.

KEISHA
(angry)
You ain't the only one momma.

MS. GLORIA
(holding BRIANA)
Now you two cut that out now.

YVETTE PARKER
(angry)
Cut it out, for what momma, he hit my daughter and what makes it so bad she's pregnant, I know what I'm about to do, I'm about to call the police on that nigga.

(Before YVETTE PARKER grabbed the phone, the phone rang, then MS. GLORIA brings up the phone

MS. GLORIA
(talking on the phone)
Hello, you got some nerve to call my house after what you did.

(BRIANA raise her head off MS. GLORIA'S shoulder and looks toward her mother)

BRIANA
(crying)
Momma, is that CALVIN.

(YVETTE PARKER didn't pay her daughter any attention and she kept talking on the phone)

YVETTE PARKER
(talking on the phone)
No, Briana cannot come to the phone right now, and don't apologize Calvin because I'm not trying to hear it, where you at anyway, you're in jail, that's good you just saved me a phone call.

BRIANA
(crying)
He's in jail.

(BRIANA gets up from the couch and ran toward where her mother was)

YVETTE PARKER
(holding the phone)
Get back BRIANA.

BRIANA
(begging to her momma)
Please let me talk to Calvin, please.

YVETTE PARKER
No Briana, you don't need to talk to this lowlife.

MS. GLORIA
Yvette, let's her talk to the boy.

YVETTE PARKER
But momma.

MS. GLORIA
Yvette, they are just talking on the phone.

(YVETTE PARKER looks at MS. GLORIA then she looks back at BRIANA)

MS. GLORIA
(holding the phone)
Ok Briana, you got two minutes to talk.

(YVETTE PARKER gives BRIANA the telephone; BRIANA starts wiping the tears from her face and she starts talking to CALVIN on the phone)

BRIANA
(talking on the phone, crying)
CALVIN, what'cha doing in jail, say what, you was at the wrong place at the wrong time, don't worry baby, I'll be down there in a few minutes to come bail you out.

YVETTE PARKER
No the hell you won't.

(YVETTE PARKER takes the phone from BRIANA and hangs it up)

BRIANA
(crying)
What you do that for ma?

YVETTE PARKER
Briana, I don't want you seeing that boy anymore.

BRIANA
Say what, I can't do that momma, I love him.

YVETTE PARKER
Well you better love somebody else.

BRIANA
(crying)
But momma.

YVETTE PARKER
(talking to BRIANA)
But momma nothing, now you stay away from that boy, momma knows what best, you don't need him to help you take care of that child, that's what we are here for, we going make it through this I promise you.

(BRIANA and YVETTE PARKER look at each other for a while)

YVETTE PARKER
Now you go sit down on the couch for a while and relax, Keisha help me find my blood pressure bills, I know there in the kitchen somewhere.

KEISHA
Yes momma.

*(KEISHA and YVETTE PARKER walk in the kitchen; BRI-
ANA sat on the couch beside MS. GLORIA; MS. GLORIA
looks and saw how upset her granddaughter was)*

MS. GLORIA
You're alright child.

BRIANA
(upset)
*Nall Grandma, I ain't alright, I miss Calvin, like I told mom-
ma, I love him, I need him.*

*(MS. GLORIA just looks at BRIANA for a while and she knew
what she had to do; MS. GLORIA gets up from the couch and
walks up toward the door)*

BRIANA
Where you going grandma?

MS. GLORIA
I just need some fresh air sweetie, I'll be back.

*(MS. GLORIA walks out the door and BRIANA sits on the
couch and starts to put her hands over her eyes and started back
crying)*

SCENE 15
JAILBIRD

(Takes place at the county jail; KILO and CALVIN are sitting back to back on a bench; SNOOKY is walking around in paces paranoid as hell while BABY DEE and LIL' SMURF and playing jacks in the corner because the police took their dice)

CALVIN
You know what Kilo, this is all your fault.

KILO
My fault, how is it your fault.

CALVIN
How the hell you gone get your drug supply from a cop, you hate the police?

KILO
How was I suppose to know he was gonna get caught, and I sho didn't know he was gone snitch me out either.

CALVIN
Whateva mane, like I said, this is all your fault.

KILO
Don't start Calvin, you act like you never been to jail before.

CALVIN
That's the point Kilo, I'm tired of going to jail for something you did, I bet my jail record is longer than my ....

KILO
Don't say it cuz, and what you mean you're too old, you only 17
cuz, and stop walking back and forth Snooky damn, what the
hell is wrong with you.

(SNOOKY walks up toward KILO and grabs him)

SNOOKY
(paranoid)
I can't help it mane, I'm scared.

KILO
Jail ain't that bad Snook

SNOOKY
(paranoid)
It ain't that cuz, I feel safe in here, It's my momma dude, I told
her that I would stay outta trouble, if she finds out I'm in jail
again, she gone beat the hell outta me, or yet kick me out the
house, I can't get kicked out the house mane, I can't.

(KILO stands up, grabs SNOOKY and then starts shaking him
and slapping him a couple of times)

KILO
(grabs Snooky)
Snap out of it mane, just take a deep breath cuz.

SNOOKY
(paranoid)
Aight Aight

(SNOOKY takes a deep breath and then he kept breathing hard)

KILO
All I see this ain't go work, hold on for a second Snook.

(KILO went into his pocket and takes out a blunt and a lighter)

KILO
(holding the blunt and lighter)
I snuck this in without the cops knowin; take one long hit of this,
I call this highway to heaven my friend.

*(KILO gave the blunt and lighter to SNOOKY and he blaze
it up, takes one long hit and gave the blunt and lighter back to
KILO; SNOOKY'S eyes opens wide and he walks back to his
corner; KILO sat back down beside CALVIN, blew the fire off
the blunt and put the blunt and lighter back in his pocket)*

CALVIN
(talking to KILO)
What was that you gave Snooky?

KILO
Just some angel dust, to calm his nervous you know.

CALVIN
I should've known.

KILO
Now, what we were talking about at first.

*(CALVIN looks at KILO; then CALVIN saw DET. BIGGS and
a big dude came toward the cage door; CALVIN gets up and
walks toward BIGGS)*

CALVIN
Hey Biggs, did someone post bail for me.

DET. BIGGS
Nall Calvin, I'm just bringing in ya'll new roommate, his name
is Sweetchucks.

(DET. BIGGS opens the door and the convict enters the cell; CALVIN saw how big SWEETCHUCKS was and he went and sat back down, everybody in the cell looks scared except for KILO; DET. BIGGS closes the door with the key and leaves)

SWEETCHUCKS
(talking to the gang)
Now, which one of you ladies are going to wash my draws.

(SWEETCHUCKS looks at BABY DEE and LIL' SMURF playing jacks; the boys stop playing jacks and looks at SWEET-CHUCKS)

BABY DEE
(scared)
Hey dude, don't look at me.

LIL' SMURF
(scared)
Yeah, I don't even wash my own draws.

BABY DEE
Say what Smurf

(LIL' SMURF starts looking crazy in the face)

(SWEETCHUCKS turns away from the boys and turns his attention on SNOOKY in the corner; SWEETCHUCKS walks toward SNOOKY who was not normal)

SWEETCHUCKS
How about you, you look like you'll make a good girlfriend.

(SNOOKY was in another world because he had his mouth wide open and his eyes open just looking retarded)

SWEETCHUCKS
Nall, I don't mess with retarded people.

(SWEETCHUCKS *then turns his attention to CALVIN and KILO who were sitting on the bench)*

SWEETCHUCKS
So I guess that leaves you two ladies then.

(KILO *stands up from the bench and walks in front of SWEET-CHUCKS)*

KILO
Hey cuz, I ain't down to be nobody girlfriend and I sho' ain't washing your nasty draws.

(CALVIN *gets up and gets between SWEETCHUCKS and KILO trying to break it up)*

CALVIN
(pushing KILO back)
Kilo, what's wrong with you mane, I'm sorry about my friend Mr. Sweetchucks but he has a little temper, his mind kind of mess up so if you would please forgive him about what he just said.

(SWEETCHUCKS *looks at CALVIN up and down)*

SWEETCHUCKS
What about you?

CALVIN
(looking at SWEETCHUCKS)
What about me, nall you wouldn't want me cuz, see I'm a little dude and you probably would want somebody bigger like a foot-ball player or maybe Snooky over there, he's a nice size.

(CALVIN points at SNOOKY would is still in a dazed)

SWEETCHUCKS
Nall, two big people getting together might start a fire, how bout you though

(SWEETCHUCKS then picks CALVIN up)

CALVIN
(yelling)
Hey Dude, what you doing.

SWEETCHUCKS
(holding CALVIN in the air)
You as light as a baby, I like that.

CALVIN
(scared)
C'mon dude, you don't wanna do this mane.

(The angel dust got to SNOOKY because he got up from the corner and started walking around with his eyes wide open and his mouth wide open, he walks around looking retarded for a few seconds and he fell out on the floor)

CALVIN
(still in the air)
I guess the dust got to him.

LIL SMURF
(shocked)
Oh my god, did Snook overdose.

(Then Snooky farts and starts smiling, then everybody starts covering their noses and making ugly faces)

BABY DEE
(holding his nose)
Dang Snook, You one nasty mother....

LIL SMURF
(holding his nose)
Hold on Dee, I think I'm bout to choke to death, I can't hardly breath, I need oxygen

BABY DEE
Let go of your nose fool.

(SWEETCHUCKS, still holding CALVIN in the air, turns his head away from SNOOKY and looks back at CALVIN; CALVIN saw how SWEETCHUCKS was looking at him)

CALVIN
(scared)
Oh hell nall

(KILO then face up toward SWEETCHUCKS)

KILO
Why don't you put dude down and try to mess with somebody your own size, or are you too scared.

(After KILO said that, SWEETCHUCKS puts CALVIN down and focus on KILO)

CALVIN
Kilo, don't do what I think you go do.

KILO
(face up toward SWEETCHUCKS)
Step back Calvin, I don't need your help.

(KILO pushes CALVIN out of the way and stands face to face with SWEETCHUCKS)

CALVIN
Step back, mane dude is gonna kill you lo.

KILO
I've been in prison for a year so I think I can take care of myself.

CALVIN
But Kilo…..

KILO
(angry)
But what, what is it Cal, you want me to change my attitude, change the way I am, hell nall, this is me Calvin, this is how I'm gonna stay, I ain't changing, not for you, not for nobody, I'm a dope boy for life, that's how I am, I'm gone die hustlin' cuz.

DET. BIGGS
(yelled)
CALVIN WILKINS.

(Before CALVIN could say anything else, DET. BIGGS walks up toward the bars and opens the door)

DET. BIGGS
You posted bail Calvin, you're free to go.

CALVIN
Fo' real.

DET. BIGGS
Yeah, come on Calvin.

(CALVIN looks at his friend KILO)

KILO
(talking to CALVIN)
Gone head Cal, gone head with Briana and her family, that's where you wanna be, but just remember, we just had each other we were coming up in the game.

(CALVIN pauses for a seconds, then looks at KILO)

CALVIN
(talking to KILO)
I know, but it got to the point where one of use was tired of playing the same old games, take care my brother.

(CALVIN looks at KILO one last time, then walks out the cell and BIGGS closes the door)

SCENE 16
CALVIN COMES HOME

*(Takes place over BRIANA'S house; MS. GLORIA opens the
door and walks in the house and CALVIN follows behind her)*

CALVIN
Thanks for posting bail for me Ms. Gloria; I really appreciate it.

MS. GLORIA
(talking to CALVIN)
*Listen Calvin, the only reason why I posted bail for you was
because my grandbaby needed you, we cool and all Calvin and I
haven't had any problems from you until now but if you lay your
hands back on Briana, you won't live to regret it, you better start
praying to God and you better be lucky that I forgave you cuz if
not, I would have done some thangs to ya boy cuz I can stick and
move Cal, I'm like Mike Tyson, I will bite yo ear off.*

(MS. GLORIA then starts moving swinging her arms like a boxer)

CALVIN
*I know Ms. Gloria and I can't blame you for that, I'm really, re-
ally, sorry for all the problems that I caused you and your family,
you guys took me in when I didn't have a place to stay and you
treated me like I was part of the family, and you Ms. Gloria, you
were like the mother I never had.*

MS. GLORIA
(looks at CALVIN)
Sucking up doesn't get you anywhere.

(CALVIN then puts his head down)

MS. GLORIA
(smiling)
Straighten your head up Calvin and give me a hug?

(CALVIN raises his head up and starts smiling and hugs
MS. GLORIA; They hugged for a couple of seconds and then
YVETTE PARKER came in the living room carrying a shotgun
and KEISHA was behind her)

YVETTE PARKER
(holding the shotgun)
Stand back momma.

(CALVIN and MS. GLORIA stop hugging and MS. GLORIA
stands in front of CALVIN; CALVIN is scared as hell)

MS. GLORIA
(yelling)
Yvette, what is wrong with you, have you lost your damn mind?

YVETTE PARKER
(holding the shotgun)
This is only right momma; Calvin deserves it.

KEISHA
Yeah momma, pop a cap in his ass.

(YVETTE PARKER looks back at KEISHA)

KEISHA
I mean butt.

MS. GLORIA
(protecting CALVIN)
Now Yvette, think about what you fittin' do.

> YVETTE PARKER
> *(holding the shotgun)*
> I thought about it momma, see I'm a lawyer, I can beat my own murder case.

> MS. GLORIA
> *(protecting CALVIN)*
> Yvette, put the gun down.

> YVETTE PARKER
> *(holding the shotgun)*
> Don't make it harder than it is momma.

> MS. GLORIA
> *(protecting CALVIN)*
> Please Yvette, he's only a boy, it's not worth taking his life, think about Briana for a chance, think about her child, the child needs a father in their life, your father wasn't there for you and your husband wasn't there for your daughters, but please Yvette, please if you have a heart, let Calvin be there for his child.

(After hearing what MS. GLORIA had said, YVETTE PARKER starts crying and she slowly laid the gun on the floor; MS. GLORIA left CALVIN and went toward her daughter and they started hugging and crying; then KEISHA got emotional and walks toward MS. GLORIA and YVETTE PARKER and they started hugging and crying together; Calvin just looks)

(After they hugged for a while, they let each other go; then MS. GLORIA picks up the shotgun from the floor)

> MS. GLORIA
> *(talking to KEISHA and MS. GLORIA)*
> C'mon girls, let's head to the back, I'll tell Briana you're here Calvin.

(MS. GLORIA, YVETTE PARKER, and KEISHA leaves; CAL-

*VIN watches as the ladies leave and then he got on both knees
and fell to the floor and starts praying to GOD)*

CALVIN
(praying to GOD)
*God, it's me Calvin, I know that I don't talk to you that much
but there are a few things that are flowing through my head,
I have a drug problem God and I'm afraid what it might lead
me too, just help me through this lord, help me defeat this evil
addiction that I have for drugs, I wanna be a good person Lord I
really do, I wanna be there for Bri and I wanna be there for my
child, so please Lord, help me through this dilemma.*

*(CALVIN stops talking then he closes his eyes and starts praying;
then BRIANA enters the living room)*

BRIANA
Calvin

*(CALVIN looks up and there stood BRIANA; then he gets up
from the floor and walks toward her)*
CALVIN
Bri Bri, I'm sorry for....

*(But before CALVIN could get through with what he had to say,
BRIANA slaps him; CALVIN looks at BRIANA and starts rubbing his cheek)*

CALVIN
(holding his jaw)
I deserve that, I really did.

BRIANA
(upset)
*You put me through hell today Calvin, you just don't know how
much you hurt me.*

(CALVIN looks at BRIANA and a tear roll down his eye)

CALVIN
(upset)

I know Bri and hurting you is the last thing that I'd want to do, I'm truly sorry for everything I put you though and I'm gonna change. I just want you to know that I'm through with drugs, I'm through smoking, and I wanna take care of my responsibilities like a man, like you said, we need to support each other, I just hope that you can forgive me.

BRIANA
(crying)

Why should I believe you huh, how can I trust you Calvin, you hurt me so, I dedicated everything in this relationship and look how you treated me, you lied to me, how can I ever trust you again, do you wanna die on these streets Cal cuz that's what gonna happen if you keep messing with this dope.

(BRIANA puts her head down for a second, then CALVIN walks closer to her)

CALVIN
(upset)

Bay, I made a mistake, all I can say is that I wanna make this work, I can't live without you, you are apart of me, without you I can't feel complete. I know what I did was wrong and if I have to beg and plead for the rest of my life for your forgiveness, then I will, I made a mistake and I need help, I will seek all the counseling and therapy that is to offer baby because you are more important to me than any drug in this world.

(BRIANA looks at CALVIN for a while and starts crying and she hugs him)

CALVIN
(hugging BRIANA)
I love you BRIANA.

BRIANA
(crying)
I love you too Calvin but next time you hit me I will kill you.

CALVIN
(hugging BRIANA and smiling with joy)
Ok baby, It will neva ever happen again.

(CALVIN and BRIANA kissed for a long time)

SCENE 17
A BABY IS BORN!

(Takes place three months later at the hospital; BRIANA is in the hospital bed holding her baby boy while KEISHA, YVETTE PARKER, and MS. GLORIA are standing over her; DR. PERRY is near the hospital bed)

MS. GLORIA
(smiling)
Oh, what a pretty little baby boy, he gets his looks from his great-grandma, yes he do, I can't believe it, I'm a great-grandma, that makes me seem old.

KEISHA
Oh, he's so precious, makes me wanna have a baby.

(YVETTE PARKER looks at KEISHA)

KEISHA
I'm just playing momma.

YVETTE PARKER
You better be, c'mon Briana, let me hold my grandbaby for a second.

(BRIANA gave her baby to YVETTE PARKER and she walks around the room holding her grandson)

DR. PERRY
How you feeling Briana?

BRIANA
(tired)
Whew, I'm a little tired right now doctor.

DR. PERRY
You just need some rest and you'll be fine.

KEISHA
Hey, where's Calvin, he should be here by now.

MS. GLORIA
He's coming Keisha, he's just a little late that's all.

*(After MS. GLORIA said that, DET. BIGGS and CALVIN
came in the hospital room)*

KEISHA
It's about time Calvin, where have you been.

CALVIN
*Sorry I'm late ya'll, my drug counselor held me up too long and I
had to find a ride up here.*

DET. BIGGS
Luckily, I was around to bring him up here.

*(MS. GLORIA and KEISHA walks toward CALVIN; MS.
GLORIA hugs CALVIN)*

MS. GLORIA
(hugging CALVIN)
It's good to see ya Calvin.

CALVIN
(hugging MS. GLORIA)
You too Ms. Gloria

(MS. GLORIA and CALVIN stop hugging, then CALVIN looks at KEISHA)

KEISHA
I might as well, give me a hug.

(CALVIN and KEISHA starts hugging)

KEISHA
(hugging CALVIN)
You better take good care of my nephew, you hear me.

CALVIN
(hugging KEISHA)
I hear you Keisha, and I will.

(CALVIN looks at YVETTE PARKER carrying his child; YVETTE PARKER looks at CALVIN and walks toward him holding the child; YVETTE PARKER looked at CALVIN and smile)

YVETTE PARKER
(smiling)
Here's your baby boy.

(YVETTE PARKER gives the baby to CALVIN and CALVIN starts looking and smiling at his child)

YVETTE PARKER
(smiling)
Welcome to the family Calvin, I wouldn't have it any other way.

(YVETTE PARKER smiles at CALVIN and he smiles back)

DET. BIGGS
I got a surprise for you too Calvin.

CALVIN
What is it Biggs?

(DET. BIGGS opens the door)

DET. BIGGS
(yelled though the door)
Come on in.

(MILSAP walks in the hospital room looking so fresh and so clean; CALVIN was shock to see how clean MILSAP was; MILSAP walks toward CALVIN)

CALVIN
(shock)
Milsap, is that you.

MILSAP
(shuttering)
Yeah it's me, the one and only.

CALVIN
Man, you looking good cuz, what you doing up here.

MILSAP
(shuttering)
I just came to say thank you Calvin.

CALVIN
(looking confuse)
Thank you, what you talking bout.

MILSAP
(shuttering)
Three months ago, when I came over Briana's house, we had that talk and you gave me twenty dollas and told me to take care of myself, that's exactly what I did, I went to rehab and I been

clean for 60 days and I like to thank you Calvin, you made a difference in my life.

CALVIN
I'm glad to here that Sap, I'm glad I made a difference in your life.

MILSAP
I'm also sorry bout what happen to Kilo, I heard what happen; I knew you two were close.

(CALVIN then shakes his head and everybody looks at him)

CALVIN
(rubbing his eyes)
Thanks, when he got outta jail, he got back on that dopeboy hustle again, then a drug deal had went wrong and he got killed, things happen for a reason, God was just callin him home, he always said he was gone die hustlin' it's been a month now and I miss him, he was my brother and I will always love him.

MILSAP
Well, I want you to know that I'm not as close to you as Kilo but I do consider you as a brother.

(MILSAP extends his hand out to CALVIN hoping to receive a handshake; CALVIN looks at MILSAP for a while, then looks at KEISHA)

CALVIN
(talking to KEISHA)
Hold my baby for just a second Keisha.

(CALVIN gives the baby to KEISHA and gave MILSAP a hug; Everybody in the hospital room were smiling; then CALVIN stops hugging MILSAP and YVETTE PARKER gave the baby back to CALVIN)

DR. PERRY
I think we should let Briana rest for a while.

*(YVETTE PARKER, MS. GLORIA, KEISHA, DET. BIGGS,
MILSAP, and DR. PERRY left the hospital room; CALVIN
walks toward the bed holding his child)*

BRIANA
(talking to CALVIN)
His name is Calvin Jr, name him after the love of my life.

CALVIN
(holding the baby)
Nall, let's not name him that

(BRIANA then looks at CALVIN and smiles)

BRIANA
I know what you wanna name him and it's ok bay.

*(CALVIN looks back at BRIANA and then looks at the baby
and smiles)*

CALVIN
(smiling)
How you doing baby Kashon, I love you so much

(CALVIN then kisses his son and looks up at the sky)

BRIANA
(smiling)
That sweet Calvin

CALVIN
(holding the baby)
Here's mommy little Kashon.

(CALVIN gives the baby to BRIANA and stands over the bed-post beside BRIANA and they both smile at each other and then look at their child

CALVIN
(narrates)
After all that I went through, I found out that drugs were not my source for happiness, that the real thing I was searching for was for something I never had, a family, now that I'm a daddy, I realize that I'm on a different kind of hustle, not that DopeBoy Hustle but that Grown Man Hustle, I'm gonna be there for my son and in return, he can show me how to be a man, a father, and how it feels to be part of a family; I got to teach him the good from the bad, let him know that the streets are not the answer to his problems, that he can always come to me for advice, that he will always be loved and never be alone, that's my story, that's my life, that's my hustle

THE END